CW01024964

SNOW

Nigel Frith

SNOW

a novel

**BREESE
BOOKS
LONDON**

Also by Nigel Frith

Poetry
The Lover's Annual   1965

Epics
Krishna   1977
Asgard   1977
Jormungand   1986
Dragon   1987
Olympiad   1988

First published in Great Britain by
Breese Books (A division of Martin Breese International)
164 Kensington Park Road, London W11 2ER, England

ISBN: 0 947 533 48 6 (hardcover version)
ISBN: 0 947 533 17 6 (softcover version)

The characters in this novel are entirely fictional and have no resemblance to
any person living or dead.

Typeset in 11/12½pt Baskerville and Memphis
by Ann Buchan (Typesetters), Middlesex
Printed and bound in Great Britain by
Biddles Ltd, Guildford and King's Lynn

To Benedicta

Chapter One

When snow comes, the world is bewitched by a kind of truthful magic: truthful because every object perceived, whether it be the old barn on which a magpie sits, or the silky willow drooping by the dark pond, or the stone gate where the roses grow, is brought to assert a grander form in monochrome; magic because in the December dusk, or fog, or milky sunlight, there is an enchantment in the colour of ghosts.

And when the snow came upon St Mary's Tower at the close of that Michaelmas Term, and from the roofs and steeples of college and cathedral both magic and formality held the world, the ghosts that had showed themselves surreptitiously extended their grand structures of enchantment, reached out to bewitch the things of the city and crept themselves into the hearts of men.

And O'Ryan himself, young O'Ryan, was wooed, terrorised, engulfed by them: strange, brooding presences, that seeped out of the stones, and lured men away from shops and safety: terror was in the gaze of them; thirst and hunger too. And in the middle of the term it started, when the streaks of rainy clouds, and the streets gleaming wet, and the bogged watermeadows by the college grew gloomy. In the damp-smelling days the spirits looked down on Oxford, and the hidden ones began to descend from the hills.

*   *   *   *

A red BMW saloon with its windscreen wipers beating and its sidelights on in the murk swerved off the narrow chestnut-lined path of Foxview Road and crunched up the weed-growing gravel of Number Eleven. A gloomy Edwardian mansion showed up against the wet, dying yellowish-tinged sky, as the autumn beeches of Boar's Hill, a ridge overlooking Oxford from the south, lashed themselves in the wind, and bowed down to the hidden presence of the sun. The house was silent, derelict, its forlorn, dusty windows looking with dismay on the day clawed from the sky by the hounds of twilight.

Out of the driver's seat of the BMW, Mark Sligey sprang with a determined show of energy. By the passenger's seat the door first opened hesitantly, and then creaked open, as a scholarly figure in a tweed sports jacket emerged, and looked up worriedly at the rain. The house agent meanwhile ran up to the porch and front-door, shoved an old-fashioned key into the lock and tried to turn it, but finding it sticking he peered in through the mottled glass panels of the door, where he could see light coming from the other end of the hall. Thinking it must be merely rust that prevented it opening, he tried again. Yet it felt as though the whole house was resisting. He put his own yale key in through the handle of the ancient key and using force managed to get it to turn. As the house yielded, he looked back to the car, where the rain was teeming down on the old don.

Since the occasion necessitated decisiveness, Dr Werble was finding it difficult to make up his mind, and the fellow of St Mary's College, English Literature lecturer at Oxford, popular author and member of the college Estates Committee, was still dithering by the car-door, hesitating over whether to dive in and get his umbrella from the back of the car, or whether to slam the door, and like Mr Sligey, run for the cover of the porch. But by now he had got so wet, he slammed the door and tottered.

It was a gloomy great house. It towered over the two mortals with its classical-columned porch, its steeply pitched roof, its barge boards and its Gothic windows, as they crouched with the rain thudding on the overhang of the front entrance, where Werble had just arrived as Sligey was still struggling to open the door. The house agent was now finding the door itself sticking, as the warpings of age and neglect made it wedge against its jams. When the door eventually shuddered and careered open, clashing back on its hinges with a sound that echoed weirdly among the score or so of vacant rooms, there was a feeling of shock that surged out towards them.

Peering into the ravished and resentful house, they felt reluctant to enter. An air that had lain undisturbed for what seemed like many decades fell towards them from the hall and seemed to die. But then Mark Sligey in businesslike fashion led them both in, and they stood together in a hallway of hat-stands, mirrors, door-mats, where the inside of the house was ghostly dry and silent.

'There's a lot needs doing to it, Mr Worthing,' said the estate agent. 'Anyone looking for somewhere quickly to move into is going to turn round and walk right out again. I still think developers would be your best chance.'

'Yes, well, we've been into all that, Mr Sligey,' said Dr Werble, somewhat tetchy at Sligey's getting the famous biographer's name wrong. 'As you know, the college had close associations with Professor Maeonides, and I seem to think they would not wish to see his house broken up into flats or converted into a nursing home, as you have outlined. If possible, we are looking for a sale to a large, necessarily rich and preferably educated family.'

Sligey turned away in impatience. He had already been driven mad trying to deal with these dons. Getting a straight answer out of a Oxford don was like picking pips out of lemon juice. He walked away smartly and peered up the stairs. As he did so, he stopped in the weirdly still atmosphere, and prickles went over the back of his neck, causing him to realise that he did not feel like going alone up the dust-covered staircase to check over the ten bedrooms which were listed in the college notes.

'How long is it since it was occupied?' he said wrinkling his nose.

'About thirty years.'

'Thirty y —' Sligey swallowed his disapproval.

'And as you can see, the house itself has not been altered as to its layout or furnishings since well before that, since indeed the 1940s when Professor Maeonides died. His daughter always wanted to keep it exactly as he left it. And I think I have explained to you that . . .'

Werble's voice trailed off as he looked into a reception room, and marvelled at the old-fashioned quality it seemed to preserve. In justification to himself of his own nervousness, he persuaded himself that his fear was owing to his reluctance to disturb rats.

' . . . explained to you . . .' he resumed, walking towards the room carefully, 'that when the Maeonides estate was handled before . . .' here his voice, as he passed into the room itself, echoed weirdly, ' . . . they had trouble trying to clear its sale.'

Sligey joined him. They stood softly together in the huge silence of the small room. A tender-footed chill had engulfed them, and the world outside seemed totally remote.

'Yes, strange that,' said Sligey, himself now being reduced to silence. 'Do you think they were really the best people to represent you?'

'The solicitors?'

'Well, I'm in the trade myself, and I couldn't see now what the delay was over.'

'Well, I wasn't involved at that time. Although I have been teaching literature for many years, I have only just joined St Mary's as a fellow, and this was on the understanding that as a Senior Dean I would fulfill functions such as this. I have been charged with selling the Maeonides house, but I'm afraid I know little of its history until now, nor anything very much about why the sales fell through previously.' Dr Werble anxiously trailed off. He was growing nervous, and for some weird reason he wanted above all things to get out again into the air. 'I suppose I could inquire. I suppose I *should* inquire . . .' He started to move towards the door again. 'But I believe the Maeonides Estate which is owned by the college on the last daughter's death . . . It's stuffy in here. The dust . . .'

Werble burst out again into the hallway and stood panting for some time, wiping his forehead with a handkerchief. Why had he been overcome with dread in the room at the front? The strange painting of the weird minotaur-like creature had been altogether rather overwhelming. And it was so clean too, unlike the rest of the objects in the room: so clean, so vivid and real. He turned round and saw Mr Sligey apparently transfixed by a bowl of crusty, snowy flakes in the middle of the table.

'Are you all right?'

Sligey seemed to be struggling to release himself from a kind of spell. It was as though his nerves were all frozen up, and he could not make a move other than the slight trembling and up and down motion of his chin.

The door blew open, and spots of rain spilled into the dust-covered floor. Sligey let out a gasp, and moved himself with difficulty out of the room.

'Are you all right?' repeated Werble.

Sligey was looking at him with anger in his eyes. 'You should have sold this place years ago!' he said furiously. 'You colleges sit on half the best property of Oxford, and never do anything about it except dither! This city could be really humming if it wasn't for you fuddy-duddy institutions holding everything back! It's time you all moved into the goddamn Twentieth Century!'

With an explosive sigh Sligey moved off down the hallway and turned his face up to the stairs. Suddenly he looked away again, and went down the corridor to the conservatory which spilled light from the other side of the house. He was still in an irrational rage with Werble. He hated houses like this, and hated Werble who was all too much a part of it. He took out the specifications which the college had given him from his pocket and started ticking off the rooms he had visited.

Dr Werble was thrown into a state of bafflement by Sligey's remarks. He failed to see why he should be blamed for the actions of the college in the past! He regretted very much undertaking this job; he even regretted coming to Oxford at all. He really didn't see why he should suffer any more of this.

'I'm feeling rather unwell,' he said. 'I'll let you look over the house by yourself, and wait for you in the car. No doubt you have a lot to do.'

With these words Werble scuttled out and shut the front door behind him. And at once the still atmosphere of the house reasserted itself, and the hush of age and timelessness redescended.

'Bloody dons!' muttered Sligey impatiently. 'Impossible to deal with! This is the last I have to do with them!'

Irritably he blinked, sighed, and trying to get this thoughts together, looked down at the specifications on his form: study, drawing room, dining room, conservatory, parlour — typical of dons to use these old-fashioned expressions! Who the hell would know what a parlour was? — Anyway there was enough to be getting on with. Well, so far he had seen the parlour and the conservatory, and the drawing room was obviously on his right, so this room on his left must be the study, just as he thought. He put his hand on the door and tried to turn it. Once again he found the knob resisting.

Sligey began to feel slightly light-headed again. It was as though a creeping sickness was intermittently laying its hand upon him, as if a kind of flu, which by restless activity he had held at bay for a long time, was at last making him slow down so it could catch up with him. There was a spooky fuzziness in the veins, a floating feeling in the head, and a languorousness lying along his arms. But then with his hand on the door-knob he found the knob seemingly turning from the other side. With a shiver of fear he pushed the door open.

With a shudder of age it gave way, and the first thing he saw was clouds of dust being thrown in the air, so that snow seemed to be falling inside the room. Then the door seemed to have fallen open onto a vast chasm of silence, and Sligey stood for some time amazed.

Coated in the white dust, which had settled in monochrome along every edge, plain and curve, the room seemed to offer a view into a world of an ancient photograph. Everything in it was white and sepia, and having lost all the colours of growth, in that dead formal state, the room had a timeless dignity. The great high-backed, padded-leather armchair sat by the ashy fireplace where dust turned even the coal in the grate to snow, and above, the mirror over the mantlepiece was coated in film, and only barely reflected the strange objects on the shelf: a bust of an ancient bearded man, rendered into monochrome biscuit-ware by dust, and on either side two French clocks, on whose faces all time was obscured.

Dust-hung curtains were looped up around the dust-filmed window that when clean would have had a view into the garden. The light that came into the room was diffused by these powdered screens, and gave an unreal, closed and intimate quality to it. Another chair sat opposite the tall-backed one on the other side of the fireplace. A table near the former was large, and on it deep in snowy dust papers and books were still scattered. Bookcases reared in their white state on two and two-thirds of the walls of the study. The library was deepest of all in dust. Row on row of neglected literature slumbered undisturbed in a perpetual illegibility. On the top of the rows of bookcases presided nine dust-cast statues of what were perhaps once female figures.

Fretful in the car meanwhile, as the rain drummed perpetually on the roof, his client Dr Werble was feeling restless. He wondered what had happened to Sligey. He had been gone almost a good twenty minutes. He really couldn't wait out here in the rain all day. He also felt a desire himself, having recovered from his fear and his peak, to return and view the strange house once again.

He jumped out of the car, walked back to the house, opened the door and went in. At first he did not notice anything out of the ordinary, only the quietness engulfed him, and responding to the silence, he stayed with his hand on the door and made sure that he shut it quietly. But when he turned round to look down the corridor to where Sligey had been standing at the threshold he now saw something that prickled his flesh over with horror.

Sligey was standing transfixed at the bottom of the stairs, gazing up at something which inspired him with great terror. Dismayed to be caught up again in the moods that had previously disturbed him, the don relived the horror he had felt in the parlour. Sligey could obviously see something up the stairs out of Werble's line of sight, and with gaping mouth and starting eyes he was trapped by the vision. Werble felt like running, but a hypnotic spell had gripped his limbs with numbness, and he found himself instead walking towards the estate agent.

'Mr Sligey!' he whispered in a sudden fearful voice.

Sligey continued to stare up at the stairs.

'Mr Sligey, what can you see?' he breathed softly and timorously.

Sligey was shaking, his mouth open, staring back past Werble's shoulder.

'Mr Sligey . . .' Werble's voice trailed off. He had come level with the other, and knew that he must turn and look upstairs himself.

Sligey tried to speak and point.

Werble turned towards the steps. He saw a staircase seemingly rearing up into the sky, down which with a pair of pistols, jerking her arms, staring, came a Victorian woman with a face death-pale, translucent and streaked with blood.

'Oh my God!' he gasped. 'Who are you? What are you doing here?'

The woman held high her hands and loomed.

Werble turned to run for the door. As he sought his way, he had the allusion of the hallway lengthening like a time-tunnel towards the door he was striving to reach. A numbing force seemed to drag back at his hands and ankles as he struggled to take just the few steps that were needed to get him across the tiles of the passage to the exit. With a writhing effort he succeeded in working his way back past the hat-stand and the mirror and the door-mat and at last in flinging open the front door.

Drumming down, the rain happily dripped off the broken porch and the smell and gales of the garden-scented downpour swept into the house with refreshing normality. Sligey felt it even where he was, and found the strength to run. He hurried up behind Werble and they managed both to cross the threshold and stand in the porch again, where comforting rain lashed on their faces. Sligey still felt his heart thudding against his chest in painful exhaustion, but he started to breathe easily again. He turned and looked at Werble beside him, who was bending over embar-rassedly dabbing his trousers. He gulped and looked at Sligey sheepishly.

'I thought she was going to kill us!' he said. Suddenly he shook himself, left Sligey and went back splashing through the darkness to the car.

After Sligey had locked the house again, he got into the car beside Werble, and tried to put the keys in the ignition. His heart thumped, he felt sick, his hands shook and it took him a long time, but at last he managed the simple manoeuvre, and once the key turned, the windscreen wipers started beating again, and a little more of normality came back.

Sligey tried to speak, and found his words came out like treacle. There was still something numbing his lips and tongue. 'You said you thought she was going to kill us,' said Sligey thickly and slowly. Then he made a great effort. 'Why did you say "she"?'

'But wasn't it her that you were looking at up the stairs? The

Victorian woman with the pair of pistols?'

'Look, what are you talking about?' slurred Sligey. 'I wish —
Look . . .' He held the driving wheel in his hand, and bowed his
head. Then he looked at Dr Werble desperately. 'What Victorian
woman for God's sake?'

'When you were at the door,' said Werble, 'I saw a woman, a
female in Victorian dress, coming down the stairs beckoning with
those two pistols.'

Sligey stared at him. There was a long pause. 'If you think
that's what it was, you've got a pretty funny view of things!
Listen, I'm through with this sale. You can find some one else to
deal with your ancient buildings. I don't know who you are, or
your friends, or what sort of things you can do, but I don't want to
have anything else to do with this.'

'But what was it then?'

Sligey looked at him. 'It was at least seven-foot tall. It swayed
on these weird hooves and was all wrapped up in these patterns
and checkers, and its face was just grotesque: horrible horns or
matted hair and the expression — oh Jesus! Like this!' Sligey
lifted up his head.

Werble saw him shape his face into a violent scream with open
mouth endlessly silently shrieking. The don gasped.

The house agent revved the engine and with a squeal of tyres on
gravel roared out of the drive of Number Eleven Foxview Road.

* * * *

'Henry,' said the President of St Mary's on the phone to the
Senior Dean, as the grey light of an autumn morning shone on a
file he had before him on his desk, 'a Mr O'Ryan: I've had a
report concerning a serious breach of discipline of his from Dame
Sonya of St Hilda's, and also a report that I called in from his
tutor, Dr Snare, concerning his academic progress. I'm afraid
they both seem to be urging me to send the gentleman down. I
wondered if you had anything to say on the matter?'

'O'Ryan?' said Dr Werble. There was a pause.

'Gypsy-looking youth,' Sir Walter Lawrence continued helpfully, 'wears bottle-green velvet coats, has a fresh mouth and wild
eyes rather like the early portraits of Coleridge. You admitted

him. He's been with Dr Snare for a long time now, and George seems to have taken quite a dislike to him.'

Since the pause continued, Sir Walter rummaged on his desk, and to elaborate his remark paraphrased the memorandum. 'An O'Ryan in whom, it appears, a narrowness of reading and research is often coupled to an arrogance of uninformed opinion, in whom a grossness in his literary responses has resulted in essays betraying a vulgarity and wildness of expression, and in whom a complete imperviousness to the advances of modern scholarship and criticism has rendered his bizarre views and stances ultimately irrelevant — does this sound at all like the man you admitted?'

'Oh yes, I know who you mean now,' said the Senior Dean. 'I remember being impressed at the interview. But I can see why Dr Snare could have come to dislike him. I think George feels that he hasn't been following through the latest ideas about deconstructionism.'

'We can't blame him for that, can we?'

'Well, we can if Snare has been asking him specifically to take it into account.'

There was a pause. The President looked out of his window, where the mist allowed him to see the tastefully neo-classical wrought-iron gate by the canal-bridge that led to Addison's Walk. And the Senior Dean looked out of *his* window, where the view was less impressive, and revealed the rather lumpish dimensions of the new quad, and a slightly bizarre neo-Gothic chapel on stilts which was in reality the library. It was this Holywell Quad that the recent ructions had been over in the Estates Committee, and the rest of the SCR were now involved in the whole matter too. Both Werble and Sir Walter were being pressed to make their decisions.

Sir Walter was not an English Literature scholar or any other type of scholar. He had — like Dr Werble — but newly come to the college, and succeeded to the prestigious post of President after a lifetime in the diplomatic service. His speciality was Eastern Europe, and he had written on German history, in particular that of the current century. Posts in Czechoslovakia and Poland had also deepened his knowledge and horror of German Fascism. As to his tastes in literature, he did his best to keep abreast of that of his environment. In poetry he read Donne, just as everybody did, and took him as the kind of model of the genre.

With the Senior Dean, Dr Henry Werble, the college had acquired an English Literature scholar who had made quite a name for himself at large. For Henry Werble had courted popularity with a greater readership than was usually received by literary academics, by publishing biographical books on fashionable literary figures. Under cover of criticism he had dished up large helpings of gossip, which was much more attractive to readers than modern criticism. Needless to say Dr Snare, who was of a more Gallic frame of mind, did not approve of this. But the Senior Dean's relish of the complexities of Dickens's relationship with women, and the strange features which he had managed to bring to the surface in the inter-reactions of Eliot and Yeats, had given him a professional interest in finding things out in his reading, and the amount of reading he did for artistic reasons was thus almost nonexistent.

'Do we have to face the fact, Henry,' said the President at last, 'that Mr O'Ryan is dim? He's Irish, I suppose.'

'No, no, he's not. He's as English as they come. And I wouldn't say he was dim either.' The Senior Dean mused. 'I would say, however, that his intellect is almost entirely dormant. I think what you have here is a student who is really not attracted by ideas at all. I think you could say that his grasp on the philosophical concepts behind literature is practically nil. I dare say O'Ryan would have been much more at home in the Oxford of the turn of the century. He would probably have talked with a great deal of enthusiasm and success to the Aesthetic Movement.'

'What I want to know, Henry, is: does all this add up to a sufficient case for sending him down on academic as well as disciplinary grounds?'

'Well, it's a possibility . . .' the voice trailed away.

'I've summoned him to my study. I shall have to act one way or the other,' said Sir Walter.

'Hm,' the Senior Dean made further indecisive noises.

'Well, thank you, Senior Dean,' said Sir Walter. 'I shall see you later in the Estates Committee.'

'Oh yes . . .' Werble's voice died away in dismay. 'Yes, we have got that today, haven't we?'

'I'm afraid so. Good b — Oh yes, you will be giving us a report on the Maeonides house?'

'Er — perhaps.'

'You saw it?'

'Er — not really. Er — I'll give you my report later.'

'So did you not go with the agent at all?'

There was a pause.

'He — er — chickened out!'

'Oh no! He has withdrawn? Oh really! This is most unhelpful. I understand they had a lot of trouble selling the house when they tried before. I can't think why. It sounds like a perfectly saleable item. I was rather hoping to clear it from our minds today, as we really must concentrate on this question of the new building in Holywell Quad. Did you find —'

'Can we discuss all this later?' said Dr Werble desperately. 'I really must go and consult some files before the meeting.'

'Yes, yes. Goodbye.'

'Good b —'

*   *   *   *

It was a foggy autumn morning when O'Ryan made his way to St Mary's from his digs in a secluded street off the Woodstock Road. As he bicycled down the High to the college, the mists came swirling up from the river, and made him think of Arthurian knights on a quest; the tower grew faint and its bells sounded distant among the stone ballustrades, which made him think of imprisonned maidens to be rescued, and the street-lamps in their old-fashioned lantern-tops were still burning gold over the bridge — but here he had to take care of his bicycle. O'Ryan had no sense at all of his impending expulsion, for his soul always burned with fiery optimism, and the righteousness of his cause brewed in him an ill-placed feeling of heroism, insufficiently directed towards mollification.

So he bounded into Sir Walter's rooms, with a confidence and a friendliness that disturbed, and the President for some time peered back at him over his spectacles, wondering if the right man had come into the room.

'Mr O'Ryan?' he said uncertainly.

'That's it!' said O'Ryan with stout satisfaction.

The President sighed and looked down for a long time at his papers.

'I feel bound to tell you, Mr O'Ryan,' Sir Walter said at last in a mournful voice, 'that all the advice I can assemble is urging me to send you down. Dame Sonya's report on your capers at St Hilda's, and your tutor, Dr Snare's report on your academic work seem remarkably at one in the opinion that you possess neither the dedication nor the sense of purpose to make the best of your time here. It seems there is a lack of seriousness in your temperament which has been found unwelcome, and that also you are congenitally unable to appreciate literature. I feel it only fair to ask you if you have any comments on these observations?'

O'Ryan stood for some time nonplussed.

'Do I take it you accept their strictures?' said the President.

'Er — no. No, I don't at all. It's a pack of lies!' O'Ryan said at last.

Sir Walter seemed to freeze, and a chill rose up through his body, beginning at the knees and slowly enveloping the whole man.

'Well, I'm sorry,' exclaimed O'Ryan strongly, 'but it's a bit thick to say I'm not serious. I'm a damn sight more serious than most of the students here. In fact it sometimes drives me mad everybody being so trivial all the time! And as for me being congenitally unable to study literature. Well, that's the opposite of the truth! If you ask me, it's not me who is congenitally unable to study literature, it's half these stupid bloody critics and academics that witter on about it!'

Sir Walter's chill had been edged aside by something much deeper and more poignant, and there was a sense of grief as he leant forward on his desk and layed his forehead in his hands.

O'Ryan paused. He looked carefully to see if the President were quite well. 'Are you OK, Sir Walter?' he said eventually.

The President gave a wan smile. 'I'm quite all right, thank you. I am just a little taken aback by your answers. I don't really know where to begin. Your attitude and opinions are remarkable.' He opened his hands. 'Perhaps I might ask you to elaborate?'

O'Ryan began to understand. 'Of course, of course,' he said, cosily pulling a chair up to the desk, the better to elucidate the benighted don. 'I'd be delighted to explain. And it's really very simple. It's like this, you see. It just so happens that I am a born poet.'

'A born poet?'

'That's it. But the trouble with everyone here is they haven't got a clue what poetry is.'

'Everyone here meaning your fellow undergradu —'

'Students, tutors, professors, the lot,' said O'Ryan helpfully. 'Nobody today seems to have the slightest appreciation of poetry. It's a kind of communal madness, you see. T.S. Eliot started it, though he's not so bad himself, but it's Donne too —'

'Donne?'

'Yes, Donne. Ever read Donne?'

'I am a great admirer of the leading Metaphysical.'

'Well, you shouldn't be!' said O'Ryan earnestly. 'He's not all he's cracked up to be, believe me, and anyway he's a very bad influence. You see, all these students here, they all learn Donne at school, and they think Donne is basic poetry. But he isn't, you see: he's very off-beat. He's extremely peripheral to poetry. He's all intellectual, you see.'

The President stared at him, with his eyes popping over the tops of his spectacles. He lifted a finger to touch his breast and said woundedly '*I* see?'

O'Ryan chatted on. 'Yes, and poetry's not all intellectual. That's the mistake everyone here makes. Really it's only one-third intellectual. The other two-thirds are emotional and sensual. You have to feel the whole lot together. Now, as it happens, I myself am very responsive to the emotional and sensual. I read a poem, and —' O'Ryan closed his eyes deliciously. 'Wow!'

'Wow?' echoed Sir Walter.

'It just speaks to me straight off.' O'Ryan shook his head and flung out his hands dramatically. 'I don't have to bother with all this intellectual stuff. But all these others who've been trained at school to dope out what the poem's saying — never mind whether it's good or bad, or what it actually does — what statement the poet's making here, what position he's taking, what question he's raising about the themes of this and that — just as though he's writing some turgid government report, with not a thought about the thing as poetry! It just means he spends so long trying to solve the poem as if it's a crossword puzzle, that he never actually reads it as though it's a poem.' O'Ryan leapt up and started pacing round the room in rapture. 'But me, you see, I see it all. It's plain as the nose on your face. I can tell every poet just by the flavour. I can sort out the bad from the good. I could show you point by point why Shakespeare's better than all the rest put together.'

'You could?'

'Of course I could. Have you got a copy with you?'

'Er —' The President shook himself, looked at his watch and let out a sigh. He paused, sighed again and shuffled through his papers. He looked at O'Ryan again, and saw him so earnestly staring back with such enthusiasm on his face that he could not but vainly try to suppress a smile.

O'Ryan smiled back at this, and nodded his head with sturdy fellowship, as though encouraging the infant President's first steps. It must have appealed to some fatherly instincts in the old man, for Sir Walter faltered and sighed a final time.

Then he spoke slowly and as gravely as he could. 'Mr O'Ryan, intriguing though it would be to have you give me a lesson in poetry appreciation, I fear I have not the time. There is an Estates Committee meeting at ten, and I have a large number of legal documents to glance at before then. Perhaps I may postpone your kind offer until the hour and the times are seasonable . . .'

But his face now darkened, as he picked up the files pertaining to O'Ryan's lapses. 'But as for these grave matters for which you have been summoned here, I feel I really must warn you, Mr O'Ryan, that your situation is far more desperate than you appear to have any inkling of. I would solemnly urge you to withdraw some of the fervour with which you hold your unusual opinions, and pay a great deal more heed to the decencies and proprieties of both the academic and social standards to which you have a duty to conform. It is one thing to hold fast to what you believe, but it is another thing entirely to scorn the courtesies and conventions of the society which supports your freedom to believe at all!

'I will not send you down, Mr O'Ryan, this time, in spite of the advice I have been given. I will give you another chance to profit from the great start in life which Oxford University can afford. But I think it might be better if forthwith I appointed you to another tutor. There is an emeritus fellow, old Dr Alting, who comes to the college on Tuesdays. See him in the Oscar Wilde Room for a Tuesday tutorial at eleven, subject to confirmation. And I beg of you, Mr O'Ryan, do not in any way neglect the niceties of this arrangement. For if I have cause, a single cause, to speak in reproof to you again, you will be sent down without any further opportunity of delivering your inaugural Professor of Poetry lecture!'

Sir Walter threw the O'Ryan papers in the out-tray, then turned to serious financial matters.

*   *   *   *

'Lucy,' said Dr Werble, as she put the phone down and looked up at him, 'I would like to consult the Estates Committee files.'

'Oh yes,' she said getting up and going over to a large, grey metal filing cabinet, 'the committee are meeting this morning, aren't they? Dr Fobey has just gone over to check something on the Holywell Quad. What particular file was it?'

'I'd like to read all the correspondence and minutes on the Boar's Hill house. Number Eleven, Foxview Road. It was left to the college in the estate of Professor Maeonides and . . .' Dr Werble tailed off, as Lucy, who had stopped opening the drawers of the cabinet, was looking a little embarrassed.

'I'm afraid Dr Fobey keeps that file in his office.' She looked round as if to check for conspirators, then mouthed 'It's not for general consumption.'

'Then can I have it from the office?'

Lucy looked even more embarrassed. She put her finger thoughtfully to her lips. Then she looked up. 'Dr Fobey should be back any minute. I'm sure he'll get it for you.'

'But don't *you* know where it is?'

Lucy now appeared very thoughtful indeed. 'I know you're on the Estates Committee,' she said at last, 'but Dr Fobey himself has — I think he might even have it locked away. I mean —' she looked around for conspirators again, 'you know *why*, don't you?'

Dr Werble sighed. Then he frowned. He was overcome with indecision. 'I have to give a report about it to the Estates Committee this morning. I need to have more time. I need to have more facts. Drugg and Webber aren't handling the sale any more — or at least Mr Sligey is not handling it himself. It's not at —'

Dr Fobey entered the office. 'Oh, here he is now!' said Lucy brightening up. 'Dr Werble would like to have a look at the Number Eleven Foxview Road file, Dr Fobey: the one you keep in your office.'

'What? Why?' said Fobey sharply.

Werble hesitated.

Fobey looked fearful. Neither of them seemed able to move.

'Shall I get it for him now you're here, Dr Fobey?' said Lucy, trying to get the two academics off their hysterical point of stasis.

'No, no,' said Fobey. 'I must look after this. Come into my office, Henry. We must talk.'

Dr Fobey was a philosopher of a thin build and a nervous temperament. He had a hollow-cheeked head that was perched like a precarious boulder on the top of his slither of a body, an aquiline nose overhanging even that, and two staring eyes popping out either side. In the pursuits of logical positivism his whole form had been wracked, acidulated and desiccated by intense intellectual speculation, and the movements of his body were hypnotisingly considered. As he took Werble into his office, his gestures were tense, as though waiting for an avalanche to fall.

'Did you visit the house yesterday?' said Fobey as soon as the door was closed.

'Er — not really. I just want to see the files before I make my report to the committee, that's all.'

'Have Drugg and Webber put it on the market?'

'That's the trouble. Sligey has withdrawn from representing us.'

'What does that mean?'

'And until there is some one to deal with us over the house, I'd like to hold back my report.'

'Why has he withdrawn? Has something happened to him?'

'He's a rather low-grade sort of chap, you know.'

'It's a very high-grade sort of estate agents, if there is such a thing,' said Fobey. 'Why can't you give us a report on what happened?'

'I want to see the files first.'

'You can't see the files first.'

'But I'm a member of the Committee!'

'If you're not willing to be frank with me, Henry, I am not going to be frank with you. We have very important decisions to come to over the Holywell Quad and I am not going to have this Eleven Foxview Road business overhanging us all again. It is all a ridiculous parade of hysterical nonsense! If necessary I will give the order myself to have the place bulldozed to the ground! So that's that! I'll see you later.'

'But, Terence —' Dr Werble looked at him in surprise at his unaccountably crisp tone. 'Why do you —?'

'What is it you want?' said Fobey turning to him angrily.

Werble responded. 'At least give me an idea what's in these files. I have been appointed by the Estates Committee to look after this, and yet no one seems willing to confide in me. I understand now that attempts were made before to sell the house, but that something happened to stop them. I really think I ought to be allowed to know what it was.'

'Why?' said Dr Fobey abruptly.

'How can I handle it, if I am kept in the dark?'

'It's a perfectly simple matter. It is a large house in a very expensive area of Oxford. It should be highly marketable. It needs to be sold. Please see about it. There is no need for you or the estates agents to know anything further than that.'

'How can I represent the college in this matter without knowing the facts?'

'It is from us that the facts are being withheld! We'll take this up again later, Henry.'

But Werble dithered. 'I was wonderng if there was some

trouble over Maeonides's will. Is it absolutely legal for us to sell the house?'

'It's perfectly legal. Maeonides left the house and all his estate to the college. It is up to us to do what we want with it.'

'It wasn't entailed in any way?.'

'No.'

'Then why the bother of selling it?'

'Why the bother of you telling us how you have fared so far?'

Fobey stared at him accusingly. The interview was over, as far as he seemed to be concerned.

'I was anxious to consult some of Maeonides's work,' said Dr Werble, as if to change the subject, 'but I noted that the college library does not contain any of his books. Is this so?'

'I don't have anything to do with the library committee. I should ask them or the librarian.'

'But surely Maeonides was a very famous scholar in his own day, and his works were widely read? I also noted with amazement that all of his books are out of print except a Latin Grammar.'

'Oh that!' said Fobey contemptuously. 'He sold the copyright on that to the publishers in his youth.'

'So who owns the copyright on all the others? The college, I suppose. Surely it would be possible to market many of his books. There must be an interest in them even now.'

'Really? I wouldn't know. I'm a philosopher. It's not my field. Now, Henry, if you don't mind, I have a great deal to do. Mr Oscar Hammerstein, the famous architect, is visiting the college to make further inspections of the Holywell Quad, and I need to prepare for that. Incidentally I shall be bringing him to the guest-night. I understand you are bringing the director of the National Theatre. I didn't realise you knew him.'

'Oh yes,' said Dr Werble with some satisfaction at last, 'my book on Eliot and Yeats was given a documentary treatment in the Cottesloe Theatre.'

'Indeed?'

'Indeed. Goodbye.'

Dr Henry Werble left the office.

* * * *

When O'Ryan, still in a thoughtful mood, had left the railings by the deer-park, he walked for a moment along the path beneath the beech-trees. The dappled deer browsing among the fallen leaves looked up as they chewed, but then bent their elegant heads again downwards. Just before he turned to go across the yard towards Holywell Quad, he saw a piece of paper lying on the ground. It was blank sheet of paper, except that all round the edge in black and white was a pattern of stylised flowers and tendrils. O'Ryan picked the paper up, intrigued by who could have made it and how it could have got there. He recognised the design as one that adorns the necks or bases of Greek red-figure vases. He had a book of Athenian drawings and had viewed the collection of Greek vases in the Ashmolean Museum. Since it did not belong to anyone, O'Ryan opened his case and slid the page in among his notes.

Somewhat cheered he then left the beech-trees, walked through the quad towards the river, and then went into the porter's lodge to check his pigeon-hole. Finding no sign of the usual self-addressed envelope that bore one of his many rejections — his friends always maintained that O'Ryan was the only man to receive most of his mail in his own handwriting — he looked at the clock, noted with surprise that it was time for lunch, and emerged onto the street outside. Gas-smelling traffic and roaring tyres fumed on the thundering concrete by a pavement stacked with bicycles in front of the college. O'Ryan crossed the ballustraded bridge overlooking the river and the gardens, and entered a pub near St Hilda's College. He went straight up to the bar and ordered himself a pint of bitter.

'O'Ryan!' came a hearty voice.

O'Ryan turned round and saw a throng of his contemporaries grouped about a crisp-packet-strewn, wrought-iron-legged, brown-glass-ringed table.

He went over and joined them.

'Well, what happened?'

'What, with the President?' he said.

'Yes, of course with the President! What did he do? Did he send you down? Did he banish you forthwith from coming within fifty miles of Oxford? Did he rusticate you? Did he give you the bum's rush?'

'He let me off.'

'Oh no!'

'Feeble!'

'What an anti-climax!'

Everyone was groaning in dismay.

O'Ryan looked at them sourly. 'Thanks a bunch!'

'Well, O'Ryan, a guy like you being let off with a caution is remarkably limp. You're a man in the heroic spirit. You breathe the same air as Achilles and Odysseus.' The speaker looked at O'Ryan sarcastically, as he sat down beside him. 'I mean, Shelley got sent down good and proper. And he was a poet too!'

'Thanks for your support: I've worn it all the term,' said a minor voice. 'Sorry, I just wanted to say that before the conversation moved too far ahead.'

'The conversation is always too far ahead for you, Ramsey! You should learn to keep your chestnuts to yourself.'

O'Ryan took a swig of his beer, then looked at it and sighed. 'Snare really dropped me in the shit!'

'Well, you're not his type.'

'It takes all sorts to make a world. Just because some one finds deconstructionism a mindless bore, there's no need to send him down.'

'Well, you did punch a porter at St Hilda's too.'

O'Ryan shrugged.

'Well! You're a savage, O'Ryan. St Mary's doesn't like savages. It has a tradition of discreet and aristocratic charm and easy-goingness.'

'So?' they all looked at him. 'What's going to happen?'

'How do you mean?'

'Are you being gated, castrated, dangled from the tower?'

'I've been handed over to another tutor, that's all. A Dr Alting, comes on Tuesday.'

'Oh, not him! He's an ex, old, half-dead, practically deceased, no-longer-quite-with-us valetudinarian. Alting's an old duffer whom nobody gives a fuck about or any work to, except remedial cases like yourself. He's still trying to get to grips with T.S. Eliot!'

'Good,' said O'Ryan. 'That'll make two of us!'

There was a pause. O'Ryan drank his beer, and began looking thoughtfully at the chalk-written blackboard on the bar, his mind revolving for once upon mundane questions: quiche, sausages, steak and kidney pie, hamburger?

'Quite honestly, O'Ryan,' said a rather prim voice, 'I think you brought all this on yourself by not doing what Snare asked you to do in tutorials. He is your tutor after all, and if he sets you an essay question, you ought to do it. But look at what you did with his *Hamlet* essay, for instance.'

'What did he do with his *Hamlet* essay for instance?'

'Well, he ignored the question entirely and wrote an essay on *Hamlet* as a perfectly constructed murder story.'

'Listen,' said O'Ryan, '*Hamlet* is a fucking work of genius. Here am I at Oxford and I get to study it for one week, the last thing I want to do is to write a useless bloody essay on "The symbolism of the cup in *Hamlet*"!'

'The symbolism of the cup in *Hamlet* is a very interesting subject!' came the prim voice again. 'I did that essay with Snare, and I found it brought up a whole series of inter-related ideas. It highlights everything the play is saying about debauchery and carousing. It is an important statement on the habits of affluent classes in society, and both Snare and I found it caught exactly the spirit of brutishness in Britain today.'

'Oh give me a fucking break!' yelled O'Ryan. 'Honestly I feel I could run mad when I hear people coming out with such brainless bloody remarks as that! Do you have to drag all literature down to your own worm's eye view? That play is probably the greatest play ever written. As a writer you could spend a lifetime learning how to write from that play alone! Whether you approach it from the standpoint of its verse or its dramatic structure or its character-drawing or its plotting or its thought, it is a gold-mine. I've got one week to study it in. Do I have to spend the week solemnly going through it and noting down every time it mentions cup or goblet or drink or burp and then trotting off a little essay on the importance of vagina-symbolism?

'I couldn't give a shit if you or some other twitty modern critic sees it as an ideal vehicle to explain his ideas of racism or brutalism or triumphalism or any other ism which happens to terrify his cowardly little soul! I'm not interested in fatuous modern hang-ups, I'm not interested in what modern critics are thinking — Could *they* write *Hamlet?* — I'm interested in losing my own modernity for a while and enjoying the vaster view of Shakespeare. I actually think he could teach me something! And I actually enjoy immersing myself in his world rather than the pathetic little babyish world of the modern artist! Oh God, you're all the same: mundane, fearful little sham-prole-minded poseurs! You make me sick. To hell with the petty lot of you!'

O'Ryan slammed his beer down with a hand trembling with rage, and stormed out of the pub, banging the door behind him.

The others looked at each other, white-faced and sour.

'Bloody cheek!' said one at last.

'We should get him for that,' said a quiet, resentful voice.

'We probably will,' said the more mature and calculating voice of Bergson.

Chapter Two

When dreams come, the soul is bewitched by a journey through the mind's many channels. Some deep, some shallow, the paths freeze the sleeper in fear, or open the heart to warm baths of emotion. There is no monarch misses the jaunt: dreams haunt the beggar and tyrant. On a million million fancies they suck, each man chewing his course, each profession and talent supping from the moon's plate daily: the front-man straining for his cue-board, the lawyer chasing bills, the housewife vacuuming, the lecturer lecturing endlessly.

Doctors of the Modern Age from Switzerland or Vienna through gestures of deep wizardry have seen in dreams: infant hatreds, baby-faced sex, traumas in the cupboard or a baffling lake-reflected world of everything. With more effect, Ancient Times divided the course of dreams into a gamut of explanations. Some dreams were thought to spring from humours and the complexions of character — the sanguine man boistering, the choleric man fuming — some dreams were thought to come from abstinence, or sickness in the brain, or among the learned from melancholy and over-much study. Some dreams were thought to be pointedly sent by spirits infiltrating the mind, or else God Himself inspiring His chosen prophets. And some good creatures were thought to own such perfection of soul that they could see in their dreaming deep into the future.

Of these many stages and types of dreaming O'Ryan read that evening, as over *The House of Fame* he poured in his lodgings. *Othello* was his focus for the week, but he had supped well with *Othello*, and the sad time of dusk looked for escape and enchantment. So for those hours in puzzled reverie O'Ryan thought on the world, as he idly leafed through the pages of Chaucer's dream-vision, for Chaucer had written three chief dream-visions in his early French-inspired years, and the Medieval form had much intrigued him. Two were of the favourite topic: the cult of courtly love. But *The House of Fame* was on a different subject. This vision considered the shape of the universe, and of the congress of famous men, and of the confusing course of worldly Fame.

When in past times, O'Ryan reflected, all men were agreed on the fame of authors — as had been the case in the peculiar school in which O'Ryan received his education — the greatest authors were considered to be those of the Classical Tradition, and there was little dispute about the relative merits of the various literary forms. According to the teaching of that strange and remote establishment where O'Ryan spent his academic youth, the highest form of literature was the epic, which commanded the heights of the language and its culture, next came tragedy, of ceremonious splendour, and next the lyric or ode. And as for the subject matter, while personal concerns and spontaneous feelings could be the province of the lyric, and festive or political occasions the subjects of odes, national, cosmic or serious issues were the province of epic, and the king of poetry had a heroic spirit.

But O'Ryan noted how in the weird world of modern letters even the smallest of these high forms was unknown. Contrary to the teaching of O'Ryan's school, the lyric spirit was as dead as the recognised Death of Tragedy, the ode was not even understood as a matter for historical interest, and the epics of Vergil and Homer did not figure in the modern consciousness at all, albeit they might enshrine the most ancient and enduring traditions of Western civilization. In the world of modern culture man was totally cut off from his roots, and despised the very idea of Higher Form. Merely for play fluttered the arts of the modern intellectual, like buzzing cherub-heads on fairy wings. The warrior's hall, the heroic theatre, the battlefield, the cosmos itself: all had vanished in the mess of the nursery.

Night came creeping over the hills, and the shadows seen from the window seeped and stole among the woods of Wytham. The dwindling dusk flung the moon above the autumn spire of the church of St Philip and St James at the end of the privet-hedged road. Languid over the cupolas of Oxford, the green-bronzed statues and the stone, the sunset sunk in garlands on famous heads. And amber-squared windows in festive bookshop, gift-shop and barrel-filled wine-bar sang their secret songs in the growing night. O'Ryan felt deliciously weary, as he stared out of his window westward, and below the stars he laid his head on his arm. Numbness sank along his nerves. Then on the screen of his mind a flickering dream started to lure him away.

O'Ryan found himself walking anxiously in the college deer park, peering about the trees endlessly searching. What was it he was looking for? He knew that he had lost something, but needed to see it in order to remember what it was. Under rose-bushes he peered, and behind strange hollyhocks, whose flounced out skirts did not cover their thin little legs. But he couldn't find it. Then he noticed the books of the Bodleian filling the shelves instead of trees, and readers looking up at him instead of deer. He was struggling to find a book on the structure of *Othello*. He wanted to know if the play had three or two flowers on its border.

Down at the far end in the history section of the Upper Reading Room O'Ryan saw a whole tumult of dwarves. Heap upon heap of little folk were arguing with the librarian, and pitching down books from the shelves and jumping up and down on them angrily. Among the books that were tossed about O'Ryan looked to see if any were on the structure of *Othello*. But he could not read any of the titles. Suddenly he found a strange door in a wall, with steps leading up to a perpendicular Gothic arch. While the dwarves were squawking down the hallway, O'Ryan looked at the door, and then suddenly realised it was what he was seeking. The door was all painted in white, and outlined with a pretty border in the pattern of Greek red-figure vases. He opened the door, went inside where he saw a winding staircase, and heard beautiful music coming up from below.

Descending and descending towards the music, O'Ryan now found he came to a dungeon where all was silent except for very slow breathing. In the crypt a huge giant was writhing with its head from side to side, groaning, as it stirred its hands against dragging manacles. O'Ryan felt his way round the walls and tried to get back to the door, but he was shut in with the sleeping giant. He struggled and pushed against the stones of the wall. They pressed into his arms and hurt him. Meanwhile sounds of the music floated all around him. O'Ryan decided he had to discover what the music was, then he might have the key for getting out. Strangely enough he at once recognised Mozart's G Minor Symphony, the Fortieth, and then he found he had been mistaken about his prison.

For turning about O'Ryan saw courtiers in Eighteenth Century costumes dancing not in the cell but in a great ballroom. Some he recognised as the characters of his youth, for it seemed like a Saturday dance at his school, except that all were dressed in rococo clothes. With ribbon-tied wigs, satin tunics and brocaded waistcoats, they paraded to the plaintive first movement of the G Minor Symphony. And O'Ryan saw through the flouncing dancers, beyond the orchestra playing on a podium, on the walls of the ballroom huge baroque decorations: great pediments and curly-columned pillars, immense statues and marble-carved arms, military banners, trophies and trappings of war.

With a strange noise like the trains that clatter to the west of Oxford and rattle the tracks beside the allotments of Port Meadow, O'Ryan now heard the orchestra falter, and amongst the sweeping bows of the violins, he noticed dwarves tearing up the music and breaking violin-strings. The clattering grew louder and more urgent. Soon dwarves were tossing French horns and oboes about the ballroom. One he saw gleefully running round the room with his stubby forefinger shoved through the skin of a big bass drum. Then O'Ryan saw the baroque façade tremble and give way, and the golden columns and pediment crack and fall, and the dwarves advanced triumphing, scattering the instruments before them, riding giants and directing them like mahouts.

O'Ryan jerked back, and found himself pulling up from the uncomfortable edge of the window-ledge on which he had been leaning. With anxiety over his dream, he noted it was now dark. The lights of a few houses and the railway signals glowed in the murk. The world had changed. He felt a settling hostility over the city. After his morning near escape, O'Ryan felt dismayed. His interview with the President had opened up a new view to him: that among some quarters he was actively disliked. It had never really struck him before. He found he had to live with a new feeling. And now in his dreams the feeling seemed to have entered.

What did his strange dream mean? It was so full of disturbing incidents! Was it a *somnium, insomnium, phantasma, visio* or *oraculum*? He sighed wearily, got up from the window, looked at his bed, then back at the darkness of the night.

Sombrely he doffed his shirt, his white stock and waistcoat, and piled his vacant clothes on the chair. Then he brushed his teeth at the basin in the corner of his room, and gloomily washed his face and dried it. Naked he slid into bed. With a sigh he noticed he had left the Collected Works of Chaucer lying forlorn and unread on the window-sill. He hobbled out of bed again and took it to the sheets. He decided to read more of the sane Gothic poet. He opened the F.N. Robinson edition once more at *The House of Fame* and continued where he had left off.

In its unfinished Third Book which began 'O God of science and of lyght,/ Apollo, thurgh thy grete myght', O'Ryan read how Chaucer was taken by an eagle to the Castle of Fame, and here had a vision of the extent of celebrity. High on a crystal rock was the fort with pinnacles and gargoyles, wherein sang and played the famous poets of the past: Orpheus, Arion and the centaur Chiron, teacher of Achilles, and also a Welshman or Briton, Glasgerion. And when the dreaming poet went further, in a huge hall with broad doors and metal pillars, Chaucer saw the statues of the greatest authors: Josephus, that told of the Jews, Vergil 'the Latyn poete', and 'on a piler/ Of yron, he, the gret Omer'. Reading long of these writers of fame, O'Ryan began to nod, reached for the light-switch, then brooded on the dark.

He soon saw that he was high on a mountain, with rocks and a few junipers about him and the peaty scent of wet heath in the breezes. Above him the clouds dragged their rosy heads against a pinnacled summit, and it seemed as if he was in a southern country. Below ran forth a widespread dale, densely wooded, with curling rivers which ran over their smoothened boulders towards the flats, and beyond the forested vale, where eagles wheeled with heads hung down, was the silver sea gloomy with islands. In the winds that blew in that strange place O'Ryan heard a wailing of women. He looked around among the woods for the sound.

There were great twin crags over the forest on the other side. O'Ryan stared at them as they gleamed in the evening sun. They seem to flame significantly, like two peaks set on fire by the sunset.

'Do you know what these are called?' asked a voice in the air. O'Ryan turned perplexed, and saw a man with a blond moustache, smiling at him and nodding. '*Zwei Gibfeligkeit,*' said the man, and then turned from the summits and pointed frowning deep into the woods. O'Ryan went the way he pointed and passed along the track, where strange objects could be seen at his feet: broken pots and vases, and the wreckage of travellers, great staffs flung down, potsherds scribbled over, broken chariot-wheels. At the foot of the rocks by a cast-off horse-shoe O'Ryan saw a dark-mossed spring, and there about it were the wailing ladies. Six young maidens, wearing chitons and decorated peploses, were tearing their hair and beating their breasts with their knuckles. O'Ryan peeped a while through the treetrunks, to see if he could see what it was they bewailed up and down the grove.

On fields of black, outlined like forms on Athenian red-figure pottery, he saw the drawings of three maids in many-pleated robes. He was puzzling over them trying to work out who were the figures depicted, when he realised the paintings were on the lids of coffins. The coffins were at the feet of the women. Among curling patterns of leaves and flowers, like the bands on Greek vases, the three drawn figures were elegant and sprightly. Each bore symbols: the nearest to him was slender and had her robe much pranked with flowers, while she plucked in the crook of her elbow a tortoiseshell lyre. The figure next to that was the tallest, bore a trumpet in her hand and had a more austere robe painted in a pattern of laurel leaves. The third was a figure in a robe zigzagged with rich chariots and figures; she wore high buskins and carried a mask that shrieked in horror.

O'Ryan was aghast to see their grief. Catching the funereal spirit, he found himself wailing along with the women. He grasped the grey, feathery trunk of the pillowed ash-tree, and sobs tensed his lungs, tears and grief strained in his throat. As he wept a hand touched his shoulder and turning round he saw a severe face of a queenly goddess. Tall she was, and bore on her head a helmet, terror-plumed, on her arm a vast shield dazzling and sculpted. About her shoulders there hung a scale-like armour of clashing bronze plates wound about at their edge with intertwining serpents. She frowned at O'Ryan, and into his face she held a sheaf of papers. 'Do you think you will do any good with these?' she cried accusingly.

O'Ryan looked and suddenly all his dream was focused in a strange way on the four pages which the goddess had shown him. There were two poems, both in ballad-metre, which O'Ryan himself had written, and opposite each was a black-and-white drawing in illustration. O'Ryan had no idea where the drawings could have come from, but he liked the look of them, and saw that they were in borders like the ones he had already seen. The first poem was a boastful lyric of uncaring Oxford life, the second a portrait of Trinity Term in the university. They were both made in imitation of Housman's ballad stanzas. O'Ryan in his dream found himself humming them over.

*　　*　　*　　*

Opposite St Mary's College, green in rain or sun, grows the rarefied foliage of a Botanical Garden. With spacious borders and ancient trees it reveals magic nooks and bowers, and sports glass-towered hot-houses full of tropical plants. Here the 'boiling Cherwell through the park does tumble its silt down', and 'among the willows grey' gives paths for punters, for the muddy river loves here its secret nest of creeper-littered walls, old pediments and peeling Baroque rustication, and the sweeping lawns that buttress his stream, and the round goldfish-ponds that hold court among standard shrubs and pleached winter-jasmine.

The Botanical Gardens of Oxford form a rare place of far-fetched secrets, with exotica strange to the bus-rumbling edges of the London Road. From the distant South American jungles and the orchid-festooned Himalayas the shrubs are gathered that show in this muggy English soil. And open a door and a tropical jungle reaches all about you, with trumpet-flowers blowing perfume at your side, and lotuses that bloom with tough brown stems in a pond's warm water, where coloured fish dart through the sunbeam glades, and palmtrees throw up their tasselled heads abuzz with bees and insects high into the iron tracery of the greenhouse. Hidden away in the English garden, known to only a few, secretly lurks a steamy cube of the Equator.

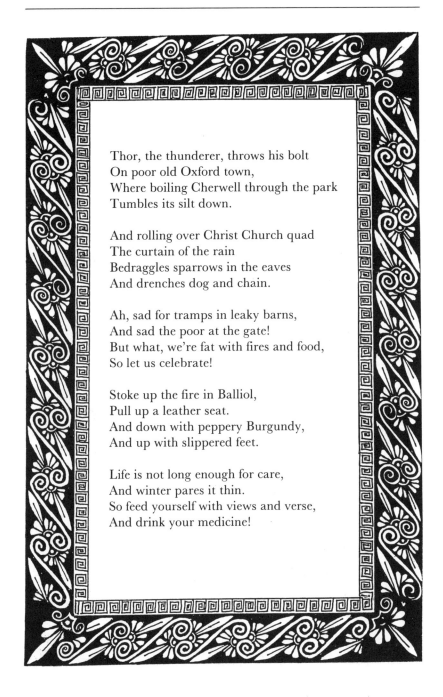

Thor, the thunderer, throws his bolt
On poor old Oxford town,
Where boiling Cherwell through the park
Tumbles its silt down.

And rolling over Christ Church quad
The curtain of the rain
Bedraggles sparrows in the eaves
And drenches dog and chain.

Ah, sad for tramps in leaky barns,
And sad the poor at the gate!
But what, we're fat with fires and food,
So let us celebrate!

Stoke up the fire in Balliol,
Pull up a leather seat.
And down with peppery Burgundy,
And up with slippered feet.

Life is not long enough for care,
And winter pares it thin.
So feed yourself with views and verse,
And drink your medicine!

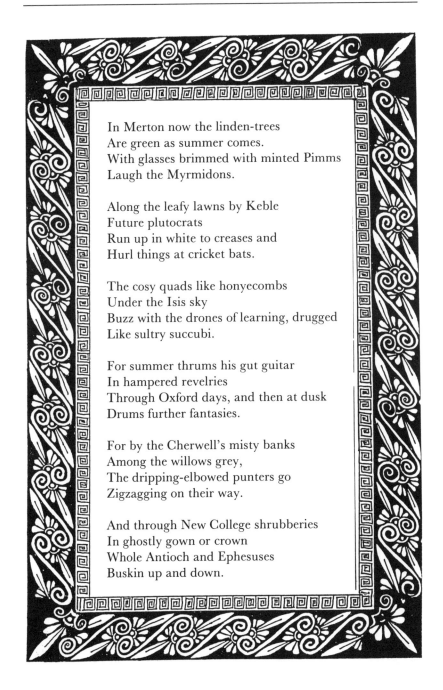

In Merton now the linden-trees
Are green as summer comes.
With glasses brimmed with minted Pimms
Laugh the Myrmidons.

Along the leafy lawns by Keble
Future plutocrats
Run up in white to creases and
Hurl things at cricket bats.

The cosy quads like honyecombs
Under the Isis sky
Buzz with the drones of learning, drugged
Like sultry succubi.

For summer thrums his gut guitar
In hampered revelries
Through Oxford days, and then at dusk
Drums further fantasies.

For by the Cherwell's misty banks
Among the willows grey,
The dripping-elbowed punters go
Zigzagging on their way.

And through New College shrubberies
In ghostly gown or crown
Whole Antioch and Ephesuses
Buskin up and down.

O'Ryan went the next day broodingly to this leafy spot, still strangely wrapt in the atmosphere of his dream. He sought to avoid the company of the friends with whom he had quarrelled in the pub, ate alone in the college, and strolled in solitary mood. Thinking still of the sequence of his dreams, and the strange sights which they had brought him, he went to the autumn rose-garden by the gate, and he passed through the black iron door on into the garden, as dark clouds formed over the trees, and a shower seemed threatened in the dull, unresonant air. With a mind full of strange twin peaks and ballrooms and staircases curling downwards, he left the world of cars and bicycles, and as if he was one with the dwarves and giants and maidens of his vision, he passed gladly into an artificial world.

For O'Ryan entered the tropical green house, and at once was reminded of his youth, and the days when he romped at ease in African air. The harmony and lushness of that place comforted him with distant memories, but also disturbed him with more recent recall. He thought of all the trouble he was in, and the animosity he inspired. What a weird world held these modern eggheads! He had come within inches of being sent down. His tutor seemed to hate him. And even in himself he had dreamed of disturbing images. Nor were the images just in his dreams. That piece of paper with the border! It was as if the dream projected it forward into reality. It was as if weird spirits making spells in distant hills were trying to communicate with him. It was a feeling he had had before, alone in the jungle, when in Africa he had found spirits everywhere he looked. And now great ancient presences were pressing all about him, and wildly out of his head all sorts of rare allegories were spawned. It was not, he thought, the Classical world he was used to from his education, but the creepy confused world of modern art.

Yet O'Ryan liked Oxford, he liked its towers and pinnacles, its narrow-walled lanes and its lawn-viewing window-seats. He loved the honey-hued mixture in its colleges and libraries of Gothic fronts and Classic spires. He did not want to be cast out of this paradise. He loved it when in the Bodleian Library he ordered up some rare book, and sat in the huge wide-seated pale chairs, with the smell of varnish and leather, and happily mind-floated into the romance of some ancient poetry. Perfumed and nodding like a thousand sweet williams, marigolds and wallflowers in towers before a misty brick wall, the poets from their shelves made heavy the air of the library with bewitching fumes. They would endure. Snares could come. Critics could twist the classics, but the text was still there to be relished by the free. Sitting now in the tropical warmth, O'Ryan mused comfortably, and the sun coaxed his mind at last to go blank.

Nigel O'Ryan, the born poet, was a rare plant for Oxford. He seemed to be a poet grown in a lurid mould. Everything about him disturbed and undercut the modern mind. He appeared like a savage with unpredictable aims. His thoughts, his walk, his talk, his looks, even the way he dressed, could be felt to challenge the ancient cults of modernity. For as the President of St Mary's had noted, he was a gypsy-looking youth, and sported a bottle-green coat, though of corduroy, not velvet, which was a kind of gamekeeper's jacket, belonging once to an uncle, and had deep poacher's pockets, fastened by shiny, twisted-leather buttons. It was not unduly odd or offensive, yet to the sensitive modern its bottle-green hue gave a whiff of disturbing fertility.

When O'Ryan was in full poetic fling the jacket was tastefully underscored by a waistcoat of a moleskin-like material with the colour of a hesitant melon: a young, fresh-bloomed melon going yellow with maturity but with still enough youth to give it a greenish tinge around the edges. The waistcoat's virginal, vegetable blush was due to O'Ryan having washed the yellow vest in the college laundrette along with a green cotton jumper. The colours of chance trump the hues of artifice. It was yet another way in which O'Ryan's greenery was disturbing.

Underpinning and if early in the week heightening by the foil of white the fleeting tones of the melon waistcoat, O'Ryan sported a method of dressing his upper torso which was unique in the later period of the Twentieth Century. It was poetical of him for a start not to embrace ties. The thin strap dangling over the shirt-front, no matter how rare its silk, bright its sheen or striking its decoration, held for O'Ryan an aura of meanness, modernity and constriction. And it was his pleasure to wear white shirts effusively tied sometimes from within, often from without, by white cravates and stocks, so that an air hung about him either of the hunting field or of fervid Parisian squares in the spare afternoons of the French Revolution.

O'Ryan was quite tall, his hair brown and cut by himself into a rough pot-shape, which lengthened as term progressed. He had a large but well proportioned face with clear grey eyes, a straight Greek nose, and a rather full mouth that hung in a mockingly curly way, as though about to promote some slightly vulgar but enthusiastic gurgle of admiration. He had long arms, great animation of gesture and countenance, and walked with a sort of countryside lope which had in fact been acquired in Africa, but which mixed with the impression of the rest of his appearance to make him seem a kind of dashing lout or cunning yokel. To the academic mind, whether old or young, the whiff of the farmyard or the back-alley — even if they had not sensed the African bush — was subtly disturbing.

O'Ryan's education had been as irregular as his appearance, since following his father's sudden but brief financial adventures, he had first of all attended no school at all, and then a highly individual one set in a remote part of the world. The Elder O'Ryan, having taken an agricultural degree at Cambridge, had embarked with enthusiasm on a life of farming, whose methods he had been fired to revolutionise from certain crackpot theories he had worked out as an undergraduate. But having married a girl he met at university, whose expectations were on a social level above those of his own, he had a hard time of the attempt of living up to her expectations, failed in his ventures, and was forced into the management of another's property: a deal secured for him by his wife's contacts, but against which he could not but help chafing. Nigel O'Ryan was born a poet in the midst of these manoeuvres.

O'Ryan the Elder was a smallish man with a big, toothy smile and fresh eager eyes. He had the capacity of being enthusiastic about almost any project that came his way, and this, as has been noted, could lead his path into a certain erraticity. Mother O'Ryan was of a different nature, came of landed gentry, a big woman with a tough stance and something of a lantern jaw. She had a downright, humorous but somewhat cynical view of things, which nicely balanced her husband's fieriness. She came of a

semi-aristocratic family renowned for their slovenliness and casu-
alness, and there was about her a stoic acceptance of things in
disorder, an avoidance of both neuroticism and irritability, and
also the collisions of interest with her husband that might have
been expected from the contrast of their characters. Mother
O'Ryan was happy in herself, and her son without realising it
grew up in the safe shadow of a great oaktree.

Before O'Ryan could attend school, or at least before either of
his parents could put their minds to the matter with any sort of
effect, the elder O'Ryan accepted with too much imagination and
enthusiasm to be labelled as a whim, but with all the eccentricity
that is usually connected with whimness, a post of an advisory
capacity with the government of Kenya, whereat the whole family
with great spirit and vision swiftly decamped for Africa. It was in
Africa O'Ryan received the benefits of a Romantic education
among Nature. In true Wordsworthian fashion the Academy of
Natural Surroundings was provided by the ancestral vastness of
Africa. The spaciousness of that continent, the timelessness and
warmth of its earth, the uninhibitedness of its people seeped early
into the growing born poet's mind, and O'Ryan came to find a
soul for himself in the spaces and farms and plantations of that
place where man first took human steps. The impressions sunk
deep in his soul: the groves of sugar-cane, the speckled, lopsided
butterflies, the musky camphor trees, the mauve crickets and the
golden leisurely savanah: they laid their archaeological layers in
his psyche. For holidays the family would go to the beach at
Mombasa, and the booming Indian ocean rolled into his heart.

The Classical side of O'Ryan's education came from a school he
attended for the most prolonged period of his early learning, for
on a return sojourn in Africa he had chanced to be sent to a school
called Dr Arbuthnot's Grammar Academy for Boys and Girls.
This was an eccentric establishment. Basking in the safety of
distance from the modernity of both Europe and America, Dr
Arbuthnot managed to run his co-educational boarding school as
if it were a Nineteenth-Century minor-county, English but half-
female public school. A prefect system was strongly in place.
Qualities of leadership suitable to colonial service were inculcated
as if to future brigadiers and district officers, and rigorous
instruction was maintained mainly in the Greek and Latin

Classics. Teenage girls, returning at Christmas to the discos and Hard Rock Cafés of the homeland, would startle their friends by dancing feverishly to their own recitation of choruses from Euripides' *Bacchae*.

In the quaint and ancient atmosphere of this regime, O'Ryan naturally grew up with artistic tastes diametrically opposed to those of his contemporaries. They were, however, normal in context. The favourite composer of nearly everyone in the school was Bach, and on Saturday nights the dances were usually arranged so that boys and girls could execute gigues and gavottes to selections from the French and English suites. In the arts of painting, since all pupils were required to study form by the weekly attendance at a life class, Michelangelo was preferred by some among both boys and girls, and Raphael by others.

With literature also the Classics of Western civilisation — that is the work of the Greek and Roman authors — were naturally assumed to be the best. O'Ryan was something of a rebel in believing that Shakespeare was equal to almost all of them, but even he did not like to set the English Bard above the Father of the Greeks. Homer — even when read secretly in translation — was to him a chief and abiding inspiration. Apart from this master O'Ryan enjoyed Horace sanely, Catullus fervently, Vergil deeply, Plato not at all, Aristotle considerably and the Greek Tragedians with an intoxicated relish. It was therefore only later in his life that O'Ryan came to love English literature enough to want to make it a special study, and it was incidentally to be expected that he would find the current state of English-teaching at Oxford University entirely eccentric, superficial, relentlessly boring, trendy and both technically and historically ignorant.

The motive to study English Literature rather than Classical had come to O'Ryan in a strange manner. In Dr Arbuthnot's Grammar Academy it was a custom — and remarkably enough a materially unproductive custom — for boys and girls to form alliances. The method of demonstrating to the rest of the school that an alliance had been formed by a particular couple was that the pair together and in public began the practice of herbal circumnavigation. There was a large green in the middle of the school, where a camphor tree spread out its fragrant branches to the evening sun, and around which by means of a special path of crazy paving-stones allied couples were wont to walk. O'Ryan reached the decrepid age of fourteen before he himself began this practice. But at a certain point in his career he found himself being attached to a particular girl to an extent which would be recognised by others as an alliance, and while talking in secret with her in a hidden place behind the stage of the hall, he felt custom and nature drawing him on to kiss her.

When years later in his studies at Oxford O'Ryan read Sir Thomas Hoby's translation of Castiglione's *Courtier*, he began to get an insight into what had happened. The words englished from *Il Cortegiano* speak thus of a kiss: that it 'may be said to be rather a coupling together of the soul than of the body, because it hath such force that it draweth her unto it, and, as it were, separateth her from the body. For this do all chaste lovers covet a kiss as coupling of souls together. And therefore Plato, the divine lover, saith that in kissing his soul came as far as his lips to depart out of the body.' O'Ryan had never experienced his soul going quite so far out before, but it was not until Oxford that he realised why the kiss that called it forth had had such a strange and magical effect.

The kiss from the girl with whom he could not be said to be in love, but with whom he had struck up one of the recognised kinds of alliance, stayed on his lips with a kind of taste that haunted him through many days, as though a part of himself had been permanently moved somewhere wonderful and pleasant. The kiss lingering on his lips and in his mind brought him to feel that he breathed fresh, distant and magical landscapes. The kiss made him feel that he strolled among great stretched-out, rainy plains, or was sitting on dry sea-rocks on the shore of a lilac-twilit Mediterranean, or walked anew in springtime through the endless fruit-trees of rose-skied, dewy hills of Bohemia. The kiss whispered gently into his ear that a warm-limbed girl was a partner to him, linked in the way of Nature, and he an entrant into paradise regained. It was in the midst of these experiences that O'Ryan felt a sudden reversal of his earlier antagonistic feelings to *Romeo and Juliet*, and this passion led in turn to a desultory reading in translation of the love-poems of Petrarch and Chaucer. With a wildness of Romantic enthusiasm that was quite frequently found in the young Classicists of Dr Arbuthnot's Grammar Academy, O'Ryan decided that he would study not the Classics but

Medieval and Renaissance English Literature.

It was with a similar sudden decision that O'Ryan leapt up now from his perch by the pool of the tropical greenhouse, and feeling mightily renewed by contact with this hothouse of growth, felt ready to set on the world again. He took a deep breath and stretched out his arms. Poetry sung in the born poet's heart. It was hot and the pool was full of blue lotuses. An Indian jungle with a lake of Krishnas! O'Ryan sighed with delight, and sobered himself to return to study. He would go back from the steamy glass and canopied palm-leaves; he would leave the moss-and-flower-pot-scented arbour, and back in Oxford, where in spite of the modernists poetry would prevail, he would relish the authors of the great forms of the past! So out through the shaking glass door he went into the air again. He smelt the cold breeze, and the rain that had dashed the firs. He passed along the clematis-hung wall and the leaf-littered grass of the inner garden. But here in mid-step he was stopped by a succession of strange visions.

First he saw before him on the pathway another of the decorated pages such as he had found before by the deer-park, and the floral-twisting border from the Greek vase pattern ran round the outside of the page as before. But in the frame this time he marvelled at a drawing. It was in black and white and of a sportive dolphin. The eager creature larked on the white surface, heaved himself as if from a sea and curved up his bill as if in a smile. Then just as O'Ryan studied it, his eye was caught beyond the top of the page by an even stranger vision in the garden. It was of two people taking a walk, but in such a weird and perplexing combination, that O'Ryan wondered at first if it were a dream.

Before him with an uncertain tread and a bent and rolling motion, caught in the sudden sun that struck aslant, a vision he saw of an old blind man, white-haired, with dark spectacles, walking slowy through the trees. And the old blind man, though unseeing, holding a white stick in one hand, was pushing a Bathchair of an antique pattern along the crackling gravel of the pathway. The old man was handsome, with a thick bush of white hair, a sturdy frame and large hands. A great leonine head he had, with a wide, friendly mouth upturned in the corners, and above his spectacles showed a quirkily raised eyebrow. The impressive

figure moved without any trace of hesitation or any hint of uncertainty in his travel.

The chair was was decrepid. It had huge black wheels that rattled round with flickering spokes, a great swayed back of quilted leather, and in its old seat amidst cushions and rugs, with streaming golden hair that flew out and fell in sheeny waves along the leather, there lay a girl in a russet-coloured coat with an old-fashioned muff on her lap, whose head and face was at first turned away from O'Ryan. By beds of mauve Michaelmas daisies, with solemnly revolving tread, beneath the monkey-puzzle-trees and the giant cedars, the vision of this strange, ill-sorted pair moved bewitchingly across O'Ryan's vision. The weak pushed the sick by the soggy lawn's edge; the old drove the young on the wet gravel; the blind moved the sighted in the most meaningful, most allegorical journey. O'Ryan softly glided through the shrubs after the bewitching vision, and moved round where he could see the girl.

The first reaction that O'Ryan had when he caught sight of the girl was wonder: suspension and marvel at her beauty. The sight of her lovely, dazzling face halted him in his walk, and swept all other thoughts out of his head. The fairest face he had ever seen, wrapt about by mufflers, hugged among purple velvets and umber coat, with her silvery hand lying so spectrally on her glossy muff, snatched his breath and seemed to make him hover above the ground like a levitating saint. The face was as smooth as the skin of dawn, and sucked oval like a sugared almond, and had a gaze as fair as a galleon under sail. The lips were intimate like roses close for silky perfume, caught when the dews are burnt off by early summer. The eyes were like September's wheatfields, smelling of grain and hay. The brow was like white sand on the turquoise seashore. Cosily stroked by fur and velvet, the face seemed amused at its own cosseting, but beyond this sparkle was a commanding purity. It was not part of the mundane world. It was the shadow of the Good in the heart of heaven. Only the cheek had a little sucked-in hollow, as if eaten away by sickness, and the white-sea-shore brow a few salty ripples of pain.

The second reaction that O'Ryan suffered, as he gazed on the girl, was love: the fire and frenzy of desire. For just as beauty might render him numb, so love dived into his heart, and quickened and nerved him with racing fire. For the girl whose beauty had struck him dumb while she stared sadly into space, now looked up amused and stared into his eyes. There was such life and delight in her laughing gaze, such humour and speaking-ness, that it seemed she was adept at teasing fun from all. And on that instant, this second element raged in the thickets of his soul, and stabbed and maddened him with a mighty yearning. For O'Ryan now was as jittery and anxious to attend and accost the girl as before he had been rendered limp by her contemplation. A spirit of silly vitality now fidgeted through all his limbs, and his mind darted to find some pretext to approach the couple. He nervously halted himself towards them, entertained thoughts of the weather, volunteered ideas that might help the old man steer the Bath chair through the garden.

But the third reaction O'Ryan suffered, as he dithered before the girl, was of surrender and resignation and ego-forgetting. For the girl whose eyes had set him on fire, as she first looked at him, now gazed with compassion on his urgency. There was in her look such understanding, such intimacy and kindness, as soothed away all troubles of his coming, as though the poet had suddenly struggled — having battered his way through a roaring forest whose branches were darkly whipped and pierced by a rain-storm — to a place where he had found himself with the clap of a door by the fire, drying his hair with a towel at the hearth of his home. And in that hearth was he sunk in his soul, and there seemed no further journey to endeavour. But then, when he looked again, she was gone.

How strange it was! She had passed so quickly behind the great dark-leaved rhododendron that it was as if she had not really been there. O'Ryan hurried a few paces about, so that he could see along the path, but found they had left the path and must have headed across the lawn. He walked smartly over to the shrubbery and peered towards the gate where the sphere-stoned column that marked the exit to the Gardens loomed. But the pair with the chair must have already fled. The old man could push so fast! O'Ryan ran now, his worries mounting, dodged through the gate, and hared out onto the concrete of the road. The traffic roared past. There was bustle on the pavement. He passed the rose-garden and peered up the street. Then the other way. They were not on the bridge or up the High, nor were they along Rose Lane.

Anxiously he ran back to the Botanical Gardens.

Coming through the gate, which was mounted of iron with a sort of kissing-gate bracket around it to stop cyclists or carts entering the garden, O'Ryan realised that the couple could not have gone out of such a gate, since a wheel-chair would be impossible to navigate. Dashing back feverishly into the gardens, O'Ryan once again found no sight of them. Coming back to the place where he first saw them, he stared about to see if they were hidden in the shrubbery. But then he suddenly looked down at the ground. On the gravel path where the Bathchair had passed the gravel was undisturbed: the wheels of the chair had made no marks. With a sinking feeling of fear in his heart, O'Ryan looked aside, where a nearby laurel tree was glossy and green.

Lying below it, he saw another page with the Greek pattern on, this time of an olive or laurel patterning. He gazed on it eagerly. He would photocopy it in thousands! He would write love-poems on the pages! He would pin them round Oxford, singing till he found her! He leapt on the paper and bore it off. Already his mind was dancing. Ballads to love blossomed in his heart.

Who was it put in women's arms
The golden havens of the fleece,
And filled the hillocks of their breasts
With harvest fields of lasting peace?

Who was it lay in women's eyes
The tender nets of ecstasy?
And made their hearts magnetic mines
To draw the iron out of me?

Who was it in that comet came
Across the galaxies of time,
Casting a fever in the heart?
Why, love, the revelry of rhyme!

Love is the banquet of delight
We hold beneath the freshest star,
And all the body's swoops and turns
Its plates and golden dishes are.

Ladies, that in soft footing often grace
The gardens at the dusky hem of eve,
And often in the grasses softly weave
The subtle pattern of a cinquepace,
Would I had not so roughly cut a face,
Or ought but boorishly I could achieve —
Unfit to tug a beggar by the sleeve,
Or offer to an ox a sunning-place!
Then from the stem with scissors
                              I would snip
The ruddy and incomparable rose,
And in the garden of the sunset trip
Among the lilies that at owl-hour close,
And touching on the petals with my lip,
Offer with heavy eyes the best of those.

Long have I listened for her in the dark.
Were those her foot-steps on the marble floor?
Now do I hear the counsels of my heart.

I lie awake and with a little spark
The oil-lamp trembles at a sudden flaw.
Long have I listened for her in the dark.

I cannot hear her yet for all my art,
And if she comes yet is it as before?
Now do I hear the counsels of my heart?

I strain to hear the panel slide apart,
Or catch her careful fingers on the door.
Long have I listened for her in the dark.

One time we saw Orion and his cart
Cross and recross the heaven's mighty shore.
Now do I hear the counsels of my heart.

Ah see, the heavy curtains stir and start,
And Venus in the breeze her perfumes pour!
Long have I listened for her in the dark.
Now do I hear the counsels of my heart.

Just as above Hellespont, borne from their northerly neighbours
in the buzzing summertime, while Germany west of the Elbe
rears bearded haystacks and bleaches wheat in the sunshine,
storks from the lush thatches of cottages, scurry up to the heights and
glide in the warm thermals in thousands down to Arabia,
while churls of Turkey with hayforks spy in the twilight
one river of white wings swirl over the Bosphorus, and with
awe tug their jerkins, and know that winter approaches.

Chapter Three

'Humphrey, may I introduce my guest?' said the Senior Dean to the President in the Senior Common Room, bringing forward as he did so a man with a sharp hair-cut, carefully stubbled chin, and an outfit in black leather which was out of place among the dinner jackets of his hosts. It was guest-night in St Mary's SCR, and the dons and their worthies were assembling at twilight, clasping in their hands the small, oval sherry-glasses that brought them the first of the glorious procession of wines from St Mary's cellar.

'Roderick Job, this is the President, Sir Walter Lawrence. Sir Walter, this is Roderick Job of the National Theatre, who was responsible for the acclaimed — and one must say controversial — *Othello* that came on in — July, was it?'

Roderick nodded. 'June actually,' he nodded again, blinking through his pebble glasses warily at the President, waiting for some reaction.

'Oh, how marvellous!' said Sir Walter. 'It must be wonderful working in such a . . . n interesting place.'

'Yes, yes, we find it so,' nodded Roderick guardedly.

Behind everyone's eyes was the faint awareness that the National Theatre was acquiring something of a reputation of an eyesore, yet along with the diplomatic peril of revealing such awareness lay a fearful disquiet as to whether it might not in fact be more fashionable still to approve of it. A long silence therefore ensued.

'We did have a certain amount of controversy over the production,' coughed Roderick, steering the conversation back to the more favourable subject, 'but in the quality press it was seen as being very thought-provoking.'

'Oh yes,' said Sir Walter. 'I read about it at the time, though I haven't had a chance to see it as yet. It seemed to be a wonderful example of modern methods.' The President eyed the Senior Dean. 'We ought to send O'Ryan along, and see what he thinks!'

The two academics shared a quiet, tastefully suppressed giggle.

Job seemed insulted by this shared joke and immediately turned to continue his talk with the earnest lady-don he had met earlier. Sir Walter Lawrence saw an opportunity to cover some other ground. 'Henry,' he said to the Senior Dean, 'I've been thinking about the difficulties of selling Maeonides's house. Perhaps what puts people off is its terrible state of repair. Maybe I should arrange for a group to go up there and clean it out? Then we might be able to start off on a new footing.'

'Er — no, no,' said Werble. 'There's no need for that. Though I'm sure I might agree it does need a little dusting, I'd rather not consider such things at present. As I said in the committee meeting, when I have done some research into the matter, I shall make my report. I have noticed one strange thing, though. All Maeonides's work seems to be out of print.'

'Really? I can't say I've ever looked.'

'You don't know anything about it yourself?'

'No. Why should I?'

'Well, the college must own the copyright, as it has the estate. I would have thought at least some of the work could be published. I've also noticed that the college library does not have any of his books for loan or reference, which is very odd, considering his fame. However, I have been told that I may look for some in the SCR library, to which I have been given the key. I intend to do that tonight.'

'Very well. But what has all this to do with selling the house?'

'That's what I want to find out,' said Werble mysteriously.

'Very good of you,' said the President noncommittally. But then he sighed. 'Perhaps we ought to forget the whole matter, and concentrate on more immediate things. Between you and me, Henry, Dr Fobey's not in the calmest of moods.'

'Who is this O'Ryan? You seem anxious about his views,' said

Roderick, as he and the Senior Dean stood together at the High Table, waiting for grace to be said.

'Oh, no one, no one at all,' said the Senior Dean, as much to shut him up as anything else, since grace was about to be said, and he had an apprehension that Roderick might be about to make some sort of public demonstration against being subjected to a Christian Latin grace. But the Latin grace was droned out by a student at the top of the hall without incident, and soon with the huge booming of voices that came up from the undergraduates in the hall, they were pulling back their large Chippendale chairs and seating themselves on the fellows' podium.

The High Table was festive with table-lamps gleaming amber among the knapkins, knives, forks, spoons, and ranks of glasses, which clattered along the outer edges of the table in companionable sport, while the aristocratic cups, lamp-stands, elaborate Renaissance salt-sellars, bulged in fat, regal silver in the middle. Rows of stuffed shirts also imitated the shiny conventionality of the upper table, but a few yards deeper into the hall, where were gloomy oil-paintings of looming lawyers in red robes, theologians in reverent black, Carolingians in satins tied with exquisitely glazed sashes of violet or lapus lazuli, and stiff, heraldic but busy Elizabethan courtiers bristling with intellect, there thronged and heaved and burbled the exuberant mass of undergraduates. As the High Table surveyed its own palatial cover, the students attacked their nameless soup in thick dishes whereon, fading from a thousand washings, glimmered the St Mary's crest.

'May I introduce Dr Snare on your left?' said the Senior Dean, once they had all spread their large white napkins over their black-clad knees. 'Dr Snare is tutor in English Literature. George, this is Roderick Job, the director of the National Theatre.'

'Yes indeed, I recognised him at once. How do you do?' Dr Snare stared at Roderick, who hesitated as to whether he should attempt to shake hands at the table.

Dr Snare had a roundish head that waggled on his neck, and rather fluid movements with much wiggling of fingers. He dressed in a loose sort of way, with fashionably baggy clothes, and had an air of a baby in rompers. Everything he said was delivered in a detached, precise, reasonable voice, and involved much moving of the lips and watery, tasting grimaces. The fingers flipped up and wriggled as he responded to the presence of the director of the National Theatre.

'I thought your production of *Othello* was intensely disturbing,' he said.

At first the Senior Dean was alarmed. He was not sufficiently in the swim to know that among the cultural leaders of the day 'intensely disturbing' was a phrase of approbation. Once he realised this, however, and saw that Snare was about to wax with the intellectual equivalent of lyricism about it, he settled comfortably into his seat with the happy realisation that he would be able to pay attention to the hors d' oeuvre, instead of having to butter up Mr Job.

Snare continued with his round, close-shaved head reasonably nodding this way and that, and delivered his points as though they were the essense of rationality. 'I thought the idea of casting *Othello* himself as a blond Caucasian, and the rest of the cast as blacks was an absolute masterstroke. In one brilliant touch you had illumined for the modern audience the whole isolation and existential absurdity of Othello's position. I found it also very telling, as an English scholar, how you alluded to the famous Leavis-Eliot-Gardner debate on Othello's character by the cunning device of dressing him in Nazi uniform at the moment he is delivering his famous Bovarian soliloquy. I must say I found it one of the most stimulating productions of Shakespeare, and certainly of a Shakespeare tragedy that I had ever seen.'

'Thank you,' said Roderick, somewhat relieved to be able to have his due, and becoming quietly emotional about the strength of the bonhomie. 'But we had a hell of a task getting the right amount of black actors for it,' he sighed, relievedly relaxing into the first of a mammoth succession of theatrical reminiscences. 'It's all very well for the critics to complain about Roderigo having difficulty with the language, but I'd like to see them get twenty-four black Shakespearean actors with the amount of prejudice there is in this country.'

'I quite agree,' said Snare. 'And with the amount of prejudice there is in the government too.'

'Exactly!' interjected Roderick, his eyes lighting up.

Ah, they're off! thought the Senior Dean, happily sipping a

wonderful green-coloured Gewürztraminer, and looking forward
to forking into his truffle omelette. But then the voice of Sir Walter
Lawrence confided in him again, and that awful sinking feeling
appeared in his bowels.

'What is it precisely you wish to find out through consulting
Maeonides's work?' said the President.

Werble hesitated. 'I just thought I ought to check out the merits
of Maeonides's work, before we embark fully on putting the house
up for sale. After all, as I understand it, the house was left to the
college on the understanding that it would be kept as a monument
to him. I need to be clear in my mind that it is right to go ahead.'

The President frowned. 'Henry, my information is that the
committee long ago decided on that matter. The house is to be
sold. There is no interest in Maeonides nowadays. His writings
were part of a vanished era. And anyway, many people regard
him as a quasi-Fascist. I can appreciate that the college wishes to
keeps its nose clean, when embarking on such a large-scale
fund-raising operation. And we do need all the money we can get
for the Holywell Quad. Whatever scheme we choose, it is going to
cost a lot of money.'

'I shall consult his books in the SCR library, while I am in the
process of contacting another house agent. There is no harm in
familiarising oneself with the facts,' said Werble.

The President sighed. 'Some one was telling me of the trouble
there has been before over this. I'm afraid Professor Maeonides
has a baleful influence! I have even been told that he's trying to
control us from beyond the grave!'

Dr Werble went white.

'So who is this O'Ryan?' said Roderick over desert, starting to
feel paranoid again, as he sat with Werble, but with other
company to his left, and ruminated on the perceived Fascist tinge
that clung to High Table ceremonials. They had moved for this
third part of the meal to a special Eighteenth Century room in the
SCR. Here, as tradition maintained, the occupants of the High
Table reversed themselves, so that everyone — depending on how
you viewed it — either had the pleasure or the relief of different
company. At this table fruit was served and nuts and desert wines:
a selection of decanters bearing silver chains indicating Madeira,
Marsala, claret and port was passed clockwise around the table.

Roderick who was now quite nicely oiled up already with the Tio Pepe, Gewürztraminer, and the Château Margaux was reckless of offense or venture, hence his persistence. 'O'Ryan: is he a well known scholar?'

'Far from it. He is a mere undergraduate,' said Werble. 'Ever since he was called to our attention recently, the President and I have been enjoying what we can glean of his strange and novel opinions. It has become a fad among us when confronting anything distinctly modern to wonder what O'Ryan would think. It provides some amusing sidelights on things. Mr O'Ryan seems to believe that all modern art is junk, whether it be painting, poetry, music or fiction. He claims that modern critics are totally misguided, and that poetry has almost vanished from the face of the earth. We have been amusing ourselves by speculating on the implications of admitting his premise.'

'Sounds like a horrible young fogey,' said Roderick with the shrewd perception of a man who knows his enemies better than his friends.

'Possibly, possibly,' smiled Werble. 'Now may I introduce Dr Fobey on your left, who is a distinguished philosopher and our Estates Bursar? Dr Fobey, this is Roderick Job of the National Theatre.'

'How do you do?'

'How do you do?'

'And may I introduce my guest, Mr Oscar Hammerstein, the architect?' said Fobey. 'This is Dr Werble, our Senior Dean, and his guest, Roderick Job.'

'How do you do?'

'How do you do?'

'How do you do?'

'Mr Hammerstein has submitted the most wonderful plan for a new building along the Holywell Quad which we are actively considering at the moment,' said Fobey incisively. 'I only wish we could make his design public. It is a triumph of modern architecture.'

'I'm a great admirer of your extension to the Wallace Collection,' said Roderick, showing that he was no yob. 'I think the stainless steel pavilion and tent-pegs are a wonderful allusion to the essential transitoriness of the Eighteenth-Century collections.

And the mandoline shape of the roof is a hilarious pastiche of the Watteau.'

Hammerstein frowned. 'The *Sunday Times* got it wrong as usual,' he said, and having baffled all, relapsed into silence.

'If you don't mind my saying so,' said Roderick undeterred. 'the last thing you need is a building by Quintin Hargreaves, who I understand is the other short-listed candidate. That man is a menace. He is turning Britain into a ghastly theme-park of pastiche Classical kiosks. It's vital to get some really modern buildings right inside Oxford. Oxford is stuck in the past. It needs jolting out.'

Everyone nodded.

'Hm,' said Werble thoughtfully, 'I wonder what O'Ryan would think of that.'

For the final section of the lavishly wined dinner, the party returned to the SCR, and here coffee was obtained and liqueurs by the dons helping themselves. Sprawling about in large comfortable armchairs, drinking coffee from tiny, gold-rimmed cups, looking like so many seals basking on a Hebridean isle, the dons gazed forlornly at Roderick who was now educating them all with a long diatribe blaming the government and the Arts Council for the suicidally depressed state of the cultural world. From cut-glass or blown goblets of various shapes, liqueurs of various colours were consumed, and the lounging fellows consoled themselves for the duties of hearing guests' diatribes by ruminating on the essenses of heathery moor, Norman farm or Alpine monastery.

Dr Werble was standing by the coffee-table, having ostensibly returned to refill his cup, but noting his guest so comfortably into his harangue, was pondering if he might momentarily slip away. He was already nervous at the President having pressed him over the Maeonides House, and already alarmed at the idea of a whole bunch of people going up to clean it out, so he could not stop himself eventually seizing a chance to back out of the far door of the SCR, which was that of the private SCR library.

Guiltily he slipped the key out of his pocket and fiddled with the lock. Staring round the room while he tried to twist the key, he saw the seal-dons still basking in the words of Roderick Job. With a click he managed to turn the lock, and then turn open the latch. He pushed open the door and swooped into the darkness, and found himself surrounded by dust, cold, silence and fear.

Dr Werble was instantly reminded of the same atmosphere as existed in the Maeonides's house. It was something to do with age, with suspension, with a deathly quiet that could only pull you deeper and deeper into the darkness of your soul. Werble trembled on the other side of the door, trying to stop himself shooting it open and leaping back again into the warmth, the torpid splendour and the comforting boredom of fashionable small-talk. But he knew he would reveal himself in his guilty practices if he did. So he fought his fear, tried to control himself, and scrabbled about on the wall to find the light-switch. At last he found, he lit.

The SCR library was a long, fusty room, filled with a huge table running down the middle and floor-to-ceiling bookshelves lining all the walls, which preserved some rare books too precious to be allowed to grace the shelves of the working library of the college. It also had a collection of books connected with the college and books by members of the college past or present. Werble surveyed the close, musty, still room, which was lit with the faint amber bulbs in their cracking lampshades around the walls. Was it the past, and the quiet persisence and rootedness of the old, which seemed to seize him with panic? He found his own reactions puzzling, and hesitated to take any steps towards the books. But then he remembered his guest, who might be missing him, and darted off guiltily towards the section containing works by recent Senior Members.

The shelves were arranged by authors, and in the middle of a fairly modern section Werble found a number of the works of Maeonides. There was a biography of him, a collection of his essays, a *festschrift* on his eightieth (and last) birthday, and a uniform edition of his translations and works of criticism. Here were his famed English versions of Homer, and of the great tragedies of Aeschylus. His structural analysis of the Greek epics was also to be seen, with his formulations that anticipated the work on heroic structure by Whitman and Duckworth. Here was an explanation of his process for analysing the construction of literary works by a system called Proportional Synopsis. Here also was the collection of his Clark Lectures where he applied the same method to Shakespeare: a process which Werble, being an English

Literature tutor, knew was now totally ignored.

Werble could not prevent himself slipping out the collected essays and briefly looking through the contents. There was a piece on the epic form of the last books of Malory's *Morte D'Arthur*. There was a piece on the oral structure involved in the romances of Chrétien de Troyes. Werble's eye was caught by a strange essay on 'The Homometrical Homer: an examination of the quantitative hexameter translation of George Ernle's *Iliad* Fragments'. Most assuredly, thought Werble, as he put the book back on the shelf, Professor Maeonides was deeply interested in all those things which were now considered to be profoundly and universally boring. Werble then saw a volume called *Return* and not being able to think what this indicated, took it down.

'*Proposition: Classical World, Romantic Culture*' read the first subheading of Chapter One, and the book then began in brisk, dogmatic style. 'All except one of the characteristic elements of the Twentieth Century World derive from the Renaissance. The science which governs the Modern Age, the technology that runs it, the financial practices on which its wealth is based, and the fact that it has been unified by European colonisation, all come from the return to Classical rationality with the bright, masculine principles of the Renaissance.

'But the culture of the Twentieth Century does not. The culture is derived from the Romantic Movement. And the Romantic Movement is of a dark, feminine nature, since it seeks to disrupt civilisation and vaunt the private artist by the espousal of madness, egotism and the cult of savagery. Thus while Western civilisation has become more and more opulent in following the progress of Classical rationalism, Western culture becomes more and more degraded in following the perpetual revolutions of Romanticism. The modernist movement represents the final degradation, when all art is abandoned in the cause of egoism, madness and the rejection of artistic skills.

'It is the object of this book to show how the modern arts fail to represent the society that supports them, and how the modern cultural mind has fallen into a schizophrenic sickness, which does harm both to itself and its society. The cure will then be shown to lie in tackling the force of dark, female negativity with the bright force of masculine discipline. And only when the male is dominant and the female subdued will the culture of society return to blessedness.'

Werble slammed the book back on the shelf. He felt furious anger and resentment. It was as though a hand had come out of the pages and punched him in the teeth. The male must subdue the female! What anti-feminist obscenity! The culture of the modern world was sick, and the body was healthy! What a gross travesty of the real state of affairs! Maeonides was indeed a madman, and was entirely wrong! It was the moneymakers and the politicans who were evil! Good God, had this man learned nothing from his society? Could he not see that society depraves and corrupts? How ever could he have got such a book published in England? And in 1924 too! This Maeonides was certainly a Fascist!

In a fury of indignation Werble now snatched out the biography of Maeonides, and tore it open contemptuously. He noted that it was illustrated by photographs, and he wanted to get a look at the man, who would no doubt be fat, smug, complacent and capitalistic! He found a photograph opposite the titleleaf. It was a youngish Maeonides surrounded by his children. Werble looked in horror as he saw that the professor seemed to have no wife and nine daughters! Rows and rows of beautiful girls spread on either side of his smug form, some standing, some sitting looking pale and interesting, some still children, sitting at his feet. Somehow it seemed just what you might expect!

Werble flipped on through the pages. He wanted to see the Maeonides who had written those words: the Fascist at the end of his career, the disciplinarean pompously strutting out his opinions. Werble found a disturbing picture. It was Maeonides indeed as an old man, and he was sitting in a tall-backed armchair with a daughter of great beauty with long fair hair lying at his feet. Werble raged inwardly at the way the girl looked sickly and yet had lain her head back on her father's knee so familiarly. The old man was caressing her head like a luxuriously old lecher. He was staring straight at the camera. He had a large leonine head, with a thick shock of white hair, a wide, humorous mouth upturned at the edges, and upturned over his eye a quirky eyebrow.

Werble then found himself reading a passage by Maeonides,

which the biography was quoting from a final essay of his: 'The Gradual Eclipse of the Classics'.

'In fifty years or so,' the paragraph ran, 'the unconscious desire to destroy the Classics will be at such a height that it will not be considered enough to have wiped out all influence they might have on any form of living literature. It will then be considered necessary to begin destroying the Classics themselves. This will be done by ignoring them as much as possible and susbstituting their study with that of those uncivilised subjects which are considered politically acceptable. Where their study cannot be avoided the aim will be to pervert and twist the meaning and effect of the Classics, so that they are widely understood either to be symptoms of prejudice or mere foreshadows of fashionable modern trends. Nor will this process be confined to works of criticism on the Classics. Classics which are available for theatrical performance will be also fanatically perverted. It will be the norm to go into the opera-house and to see a Mozart opera paraded as though in chains to modernism. It is at this point that the terrifying reaction will come. The heavens themselves will look down with vengeance. When gods and heroes are paraded as captives, when heroism is made cowardice and beauty ungainliness, when black is made white, then the spirits will take revenge. And woe to those who have partaken in this secret, cowardly corruption, for they will be haunted even to the grave!'

Werble leapt in fear, shut the book in a horrified clap that made the whole dusty library echo. And then he dashed for the door.

* * * *

'Terence, I must speak to you,' said Dr Werble to the Estates Bursar, having gained admittance to his room the next morning.

Dr Fobey looked at him mistrustfully. 'Is it about the Holywell Quad?' he said irritably, 'I warn you I am not abandoning my position.'

'No, no, Terence, not at all!' said Werble. 'I think I'm on your side on this. We must move with the times.'

'It's not about that stupid idea to pledge a box in the National Theatre, I hope? We really don't have money to throw around!'

'No, it's not. Terence, you seem to forget how I came before, and how you refused me sight of a certain file. I've come about the Boar's Hill House, Maeonides's place.'

'You're not seeing that file —'

'Terence, I have a confession to make.'

'Oh?' Fobey turned around and looked at him severely. His face set hard as he listened.

Werble took a deep breath. 'When I said to the committee that I wished for more time before I committed myself to a report, I gave the impression that I had not been to visit the Maeonides house, and that Sligey had backed out of the deal for his own reasons.'

'You did, yes!' said Fobey sharply. 'Assuredly that is just what you did.' He glared at him with his popping eyes standing out madly aside his thin beaked nose. 'Am I to understand that all this shilly-shallying of yours is for other reasons?'

'In a way it is, yes.'

'Have you been to the house?'

'Well, I and Sligey —'

'Have you been there and seen it?'

'This is why — you understand — I wanted to see the files —'

'Have you been there?'

'Yes.'

'What did you see?'

'Can I have a drink?'

'But Henry, it's half past eleven in the morning!'

Werble said no more. Fobey stared at him with grave misgivings and saw that the man was afraid. He went to a cupboard and got out a decanter of sherry. 'It's all I have, I'm afraid,' he said holding it up.

'Then make it a big one. My blood is thin from the dinner last night.'

Fobey frowned at him, as he handed him a large glass. 'You deserted your guest last night too!'

'Oh, did he notice?' said Werble surprised. 'When I came back he seemed to be saying just the same thing as when I left.'

'You looked as though you had been assaulted by a ghost. You better tell me everthing that happened. And make it quick. You and Sligey went up to the house?'

'I went up to the house with Sligey, yes, in his car. We got into the place. It was very quiet and very dusty. I left him in the house for a while, as I felt rather unwell. When I came back he seemed transfixed by something. He was looking up the stairs at something. Then I looked too. It was a woman in Victorian dress coming down towards him.'

'A woman in Victorian dress?'

'Yes, with two pistols.'

'Two pistols!'

'We managed to get out of the place and back to the car. But I must say, I want to be done with this job. Either that, or you let me see these files. What on earth is happening up there? You obviously know something.'

Fobey was quiet for a long time. 'What happened to the house agent?'

'He was very frightened. He was petrified. He gave up the job as soon as we were safe in the car.'

'Why do you think you saw a woman in Victorian dress?' Fobey was genuinely puzzled.

'Well, damn it, it was a ghost!' said Werble, regaining some courage from frustration. 'It was obviously one of Maeonides's daughters or something. Thank God, I didn't see *him*!'

'No, it wasn't.'

'No, it wasn't what?'

'It wasn't a daughter of Maeonides. She would have been in modern or Twenties dress, not Victorian. No one connected with Maeonides would have been in Victorian dress.'

Werble was baffled and stared.

'So it's not him who's haunting the place?' he said at last.

'What makes you think it should be?' said Fobey carefully.

'Have you read about the man?' Werble exclaimed incredulously. 'That's where I slipped away after the dinner. I went to the SCR library and had a look at his books: those on him and those by him. Do you know the sort of thing he says? The gods are going to take revenge on us for the decay of Classical studies! The modern cultural world is sick with schizophrenia! The female of Romanticism must be subdued by the bright masculine force of Classicism! When black is made white, then the spirits will take revenge! If he'd written that today he'd be in jail.'

Dr Fobey looked at him. 'Now you know why the college is

sitting on the copyright to those works, at least until the fifty years run out, which unfortunately is not long to be delayed. We are not going to publish material like that. A decision was taken years ago among all the fellows that Maeonides's work as far as possible is to be suppressed. Neither you nor the President were here at that time. You would both have been told in due course. You see now why we want to sell this house. Maeonides was an evil man. We want to have nothing more to do with him.'

'Then I begin to appreciate,' said Werble wonderingly, 'the terrible power that was in that house: that evil, brutal, Fascist cult of discipline!' Werble panted and took a giant swig of sherry.

Fobey was still thoughtful. 'I still can't think why it was a Victorian woman with two pistols!'

Werble put his sherry down determinedly. 'May I see those files now?'

'Yes.' Fobey sighed and got up. He went to a locked cabinet and took out his keys. He undid and creaked open the door. He reached in and took out a file marked PROFESSOR MAE-ONIDES BEQUEST. He handed it to Werble.

'You can read it here, but it doesn't go out of this room,' said Fobey. 'I can't risk any of this getting out to the press. I want to sell that place, get rid of it, so we can concentrate on the new quad. But I'll tell you quickly what those files say. They say, like you, that the place is haunted. On two separate sets of occasions we sent a team of scouts up there: college servants from the kitchen and from the cleaners, and senior members to supervise and check the place; the college butler we sent too, and the bursar went. They all experienced the same terrible things. We had a hell of a time stopping people shooting their mouths off. But nearly everyone said the same as you. They saw things. I don't remember anyone seeing a Victorian woman, but everybody saw things anyway —'

'Well, Sligey saw something different from me.'

'What?' Fobey froze.

'Sligey said he saw a tall, swaying figure on weird, high sorts of hooves.'

'With checkered kind of robes, and then a great head with massive horns or whatnot?'

'Yes, yes! And staring eyes —'

'And a great mouth gaping open?'

'Yes.'

'They were seen. Such things were seen in the house. You'll find it all minuted there. And small creatures, and very tall beings. Different people see different things. The place is certainly bewitched. And some of our employees unfortunately became very disturbed. It seems that when they were inside looking out they saw these dwarf-like creatures, as if the garden had been turned into them. And those up on the higher storeys would look out through the window and see huge faces staring in at them moronically, *at a level with them*. Their feet would be some twenty, thirty feet down! We had a great deal of trouble over it. Of course some occasions weren't as hysterical as others. But it got in the end that we just had to forget about the place. It was beginning to haunt the whole college. If not the whole town. It was like some great fortress up there on the hill, commanding the defences of the city, and it seemed to desire to draw all into its terror.'

'So it is Maeonides that did this?'

'Oh yes,' said Fobey. 'He was a complete megalomaniac. He wanted to get the whole world into his power, to submit it to his Fascist displines. He wanted to take over America for God's sake! I really do believe that he willed all this so strongly, that his influence is still going on even beyond the grave. Even though no one reads his books.' Fobey looked at Werble urgently. 'That's why it's absolutely vital that we get this Holywell project for Hammerstein. To have that Quintin Hargreaves design would be playing straight into Maeonides's hands. A neo-classical building is just what he would recommend!'

'But you can't think that Maeonides, who has been dead since 1949, is having an influence on things like this?'

'Can't I just? You've felt it yourself. No one can say I persuaded you. That's why I want to get the house sold. I want to sell it, to break it up, to change it, to disperse its weird influence, to put it behind us and stop having to think all the time about its baleful gaze staring and judging everything we do down here! If we can't get an estate agent to handle it, I'll start breaking it up anyway. I can at least sell off the furniture and books before we get rid of the premises. I shall go there myself and get started.'

Fobey sat down at his desk and began looking hurriedly through the yellow pages.

Werble stared at him, then sat down softly with the file.

*　*　*　*

It was a gloomy, grey day, as O'Ryan sat on the mould-green, sodden bench in the Botanical Gardens, staring at the faded brick wall, and the gleaming gravel path. The lawn was littered with dry leaves that had cascaded from the beech-trees, and the fusty, decaying smell lingered among the twigs snapped off by the gales. In the bed beyond the path the lupins had all gone, the delphiniums were towers no more; only the Michaelmas daisies clustered together littering the drab mauve of their petals among the drooping stems. On the flaking wall behind, the wisteria dropped its yellow fish-skeletons onto the cold, empty soil. Why had she never come back?

O'Ryan had come to this place every lunch-time now for three days. He had even neglected his friends in the pub to sit for two hours together keeping the vigil in case they should come. With a can of tinny beer, and a cling-foiled round of brown-bread sandwiches from the Covered Market, he had waited for the return of the pair who took a walk that day, and about whom he had been thinking ever since. But they had never returned. They had not seen fit to repeat that moment of communication which had struck so deeply into O'Ryan's heart. He felt as though a great mystery had been promised him, and for some reason it had not been revealed.

As he had a thousand times, he thought back on the vision that had bewitched him. The old white-haired man had had a kindly face. His frosty hair was thick and strong, and above his black glasses he could just see a quirky eyebrow. And O'Ryan thought on the other face, the face which had haunted him ever since, hugged by amber and violet and looking so profoundly into his soul. As he considered the memory of her glance, he knew that he was in love with her. His love of her was dragging down his heart, and filling his veins with painful yet delicious fire. He had been astonished at the feelings that had taken him. He had returned to the Medieval poets to try and make sense of them, and he had found like Chaucer that he 'burned with amorous pleasance'. And as he considered, with the help of the records in the words of the ancient poets, the searing power of love and its many wonders, he found himself to be a perfect recreation of the type, and rejoiced to think of himself as a courtly lover.

It had been strange, for he had come to realise that he now felt as actual the love which he had previously considered to be only a literary convention. Modern critics considering Chaucer often think he jokes about love, and treats courtly love from a satiric standpoint. But O'Ryan had come to know better by experiencing what Chaucer described, and Petrarch and Bernard de Ventador before him. All Medieval poets speak smilingly, but a Medieval smile is of sympathy, not Modern scorn. And when O'Ryan read now of lovers becoming faint, locking themselves in dark rooms to brood, wasting away, losing weight, sighing furnace-like or weeping, though he once had imagined — like most modern readers — that these descriptions were for form's sake, and were a kind of allegory of suffering, he saw now that these passages described an actual state. He saw that they were merely a list of bodily symptoms. Sinking into the consolation of those who suffered the same, he felt a great kinship for such lovers as Romeo or Troilus. He also felt that now as a poet he might wield a Petrarchan plume as of right.

But here a difference between himself and the Medieval lover made O'Ryan suffer his love more keenly and despairingly. For a while he had in the modern age felt all the conventional sufferings of the Twelfth Century courtly lover, the circumstances of his love had added a further agony. For O'Ryan was like a fisherman who had pushed out his boat onto the Lake of Magic, and there in the Woods of Enchantment for a moment of Love's Oblivion had brought to the surface on his line the great golden fish of Ultimate Mystery, and splash — through numb fingers he had let the slimey beast slip from his possessing. And as such a fisherman might be haunted by the memory of a flash of gold scales fading from sunlight into the muddy depths, so was O'Ryan haunted by the realisation that he had not seized the vision when he had the chance, and thus all hope of love, or revelation, or knowledge had gone.

O'Ryan sighed, screwed up the foil that had wrapt his sandwiches and stomped off towards the exit from the garden. The gas-fumed traffic brewed constantly over the bridge, and he dodged through the cars and bicycles, and jumped onto the safety of the dusty pavement. Mournfully he went through the lodge, checked his pigeon-holes once more to see if he had any mail, but found no communication from anyone. With a sense of relief he then left all these troubles and went back to work in the library. He opened once more the Variorum Edition of Shakespeare's *Othello* and continued his reading.

* * * *

'O'Ryan's not here again today,' said Fosdyke, looking round the pub, as the place began to empty from its lunch-time influx.

'No, it's weird, isn't it?' said Greaves. 'It must be this love-affair of his.'

'Yes, he does seem to get a bit absorbed.'

'Is he really having another love-affair? Have we got to go through that again? Wasn't it bad enough when he had the hots for Felicity McGuire?'

A group rolling of eyes went up at the idea of anyone being in love with Felicity McGuire.

But then a thoughtful voice interposed. 'It's not really possible to get the hots for Felicity McGuire. To get the hots you need to suffer some preliminary anxiety. With Felicity McGuire this rarely happens.'

'Who is it O'Ryan's in love with then?'

'Difficult to say.'

'Has he told you about it?'

'A bit.'

'So who is it?'

'Well, it's more what is it.'

There was a chorus of crude laughter.

'Don't tell us it's a dog!'

'No, a ghost!'

'A ghost?'

'Come off it!'

'S'true.'

'How can anyone be in love with a ghost?'

'Is O'Ryan anyone?'

'When did it happen?'

'No ordinary modern mortal could inspire the white-hot delirium of his fever.'

'When and how did it happen?'

'Yesterday, was it? Or the day before? He wandered poetically
into the Botanical Gardens and fell in love with a ghost. It was
your usual sort of thing, you know. O'Ryan was mooning about,
and suddenly he saw a beautiful girl-ghost pushing an old
man-ghost around in a wheel-chair and —'

'Get it right, Fosdyke! He saw a horrible old man-ghost pushing
around a beautiful girl-ghost in a wheel-chair.'

'That's a bit funny, isn't it?' said Ramsey.

Everybody looked at him.

'You could say that, yes.'

'Well, I mean an old man pushing a young girl around in a
wheel-chair, I mean, it should be the other way r —'

'These are fucking ghosts, Ramsey! How do you know what
their sense of etiquette is?'

Pause. 'Yes, I suppose you're right.'

'How uncommonly singular!'

'How singuarly uncommon!'

'Anyway,' said Fosdyke, 'that is what has happened to O'Ryan,
and off his lunch he has been perhaps terminally put.'

'And his beer too, I shouldn't wonder,' said an eager hearer
who now lifted up his empty glass high over his lips and forehead.
'Goodness me!' he said echoing in it with wild astonishment. 'I
can see right through the bottom of my glass!'

'Yes, whose round is it?'

'Yours, Fosdyke.'

'Oh no it's not.'

'Oh, yes it is. I bought yesterday's.'

'And I did too. Fosdyke hasn't bought since the day before
yesterday.'

'I have.'

'You ain't.'

'All right. Pints?'

'A swift half.'

'Lager, please.'

Fosdyke clanked off with a fistful of glasses and waited for the tarted up barmaid to finish her conversation with Medallion Man. The others stared thoughtfully at the rings of beer on the table.

'You know, a funny thing happened to me on Boar's Hill the other evening,' said Bergson in deliberate tones, and with a momentousness that forbad the facetious.

'What?' said Fosdyke from the bar.

'I'll wait till you come back,' said Bergson. 'This may have import for us all.'

There was a pause, since after this remark everyone felt rather puzzled and slightly unnerved. In the pause Fosdyke returned from the bar with a tray of brown glasses. Soon they were all served, slurped, and the attention returned to Bergson.

Bergson began. 'Since I had reason to believe from a magazine advertisement that there was a collector of shells south of Oxford who might be willing to sell a particular type of conch from the Seychelles, I went recently across Folly Bridge and up to Boar's Hill on my bicycle. As it happened I was mistaken about the possible acquisition. The advertisement was totally misleading. But in the process of being misled I found myself approaching a house which I considered to be the right, but discovered to be the wrong one.'

Bergson frowned, took a slightly prissy sip of his lager, and looked round about at the completely transformed company. 'I now know,' he said, 'that there is a very strange house at Number Eleven Foxview Road. It is an Edwardian mansion with a gravel drive leading up through rhododendron shrubs, bay windows, an impressive pair of Doric columns supporting a portico, and round the back — as I discovered — a conservatory with some wrought-iron work. Half a century or so ago it would have been a very handsome mansion. But now it is a completely derelict, strangely empty, moss-covered, creeper-hung, echoing, dusty, weird half-ruin. When I tried to ring the bell, it didn't work. When I knocked on the door, the whole place sounded hollow. When I looked in the window, it was as if the rooms were frozen, and were creepily inhabited by ghosts. It was such an old-fashioned place, it immediately put me in mind of some one concerning whose affairs we have had reason to be aghast. Can you think who?'

They all smiled, raised their eyebrows and nodded.

'Indeed,' said Bergson, 'we are all thinking of O'Ryan. O'Ryan who has to go on Tuesday to meet his new tutor. O'Ryan who has to meet his new tutor, Dr Alting, if you remember, at eleven o' clock on Tuesday morning in the Oscar Wilde Room. But you know, I was just wondering, having seen this house, and having had O'Ryan act so unpleasantly to us a day ago, do you think these arrangements for his tutorial could possibly be tampered with? For instance, I was wondering: what if something should happen to disturb or change the details of these events. See what you think. There might be a fascinating outcome.

'What if O'Ryan should receive a letter? A letter just typed on plain paper and signed supposedly by his new tutor, Dr Alting. And what if this letter should tell O'Ryan that the place for his tutorial, though not the time, had unfortunately had to be changed? And what if the letter should tell him that instead of proceeding to the Oscar Wilde Room on Tuesday at eleven, he should go instead to the house of the tutor himself? And the address that this plain-paper, typed letter would give him to get him to the tutorial would be, of course, Number Eleven Foxview Road, Boar's Hill. If such a thing should happen, O'Ryan would have no reason to doubt that the letter did not truly come from his new tutor, and instead of going to the place appointed, while his real tutor fumed and waited, O'Ryan would parade up and down outside a derelict mansion. Imagine the face of the born poet, as he peered up at vacant windows and sought to get a long-dead bell to ring, looking desolately for his new tutor in shadowy glass reflections, and expecting but not getting any answer to his urgent knocks and pleas! There would be something fitting in a long-empty and silent house giving him a frigid, speechless answer — of the sort he normally gets from literary editors! The upshot of this comical episode would be that O'Ryan would have a long wait and we would have a short spell of delirium. And wouldn't that be a jolly japing way to pay him for being such a madman, and to get back at him for those rude things he said to us the other day?'

Bergson was a graduate student and older than the others, and when he looked at the company, a chill seemed to descend on them. But Bergson continued staring at them, and there was something commanding in his gaze. One by one they came to nod their agreement.

* * * *

As the afternoon wore on towards evening, O'Ryan shut the Variorum *Othello* with the usual amazement that greeted him on finishing a Shakespeare play. Everyone a winner, he always said, but somehow he always thought that the one he was beginning could never be as good as the one he had just finished. But then a different world took over, a totally integrated world of rich, embroidered senses and emotions, and the masterly scheme of powerful limbs moved on to its riot or terrors, and the book was closed in wonder and delight. Bull's eye again! thought O'Ryan heartily. And he had read also the prose of Cinthio, and the *novella* where Shakespeare got the story. This had been as crude, cheap and nasty as the play was heroic and beautiful. What a warm, Mediterranean sea-change had come over that horrible little murder! A wash of Cyprian seas and dusks, a pageant of generals, a bitter clash of tears and damnation!

Inspired by sublimity, O'Ryan sighed and strolled out of the library, down the steps and towards the porter's lodge. He checked once more his pigeon-hole to see if anyone loved him. To his interest and surprise, there were some who did. Among the mass of letters addressed to all the Os, he found that the university post had delivered two letters for Nigel O'Ryan. Taking them up and opening one, he walked on again towards the cloisters reading. But the letter brought him irritation and disappointment. He stopped on the path that led to the archway, and as the dusk surrounded him he read yet another dreary letter of regret.

Dear Mr O'Ryan,
I am sending back your poems, as none of them are suitable to a magazine of serious literary content. Your pose of ignoring the revolutions won by Auden and Larkin for modern poetry is unacceptable, and not a convincing stance. You cannot go back onto outmoded forms which have been superseded, and are not relevant. I found also your use of language very strange. It's hard to find a normal sentence

— almost every one has a strange use of words or a grammatical error. So far I haven't seen any evidence that you can write normal, coherent English. Please leave poetry to serious poets who care about the importance and purity of language.

　　Yours sincerely,
Sebastian Cruze-Antonio

This letter, which was from the literary editor of *Isis* and foolishly turned down the honour of publishing the work of the born poet, some of which he had composed in a fever of love after his vision in the Botanical Gardens, caused O'Ryan to suffer a frequently-felt pang of anger and dismay. Like all authors O'Ryan suffered when his work was rejected, since the fire and breeze and blood in which it had been conceived had been not only spurned by a fellow soul, but something intimate and tender to the writer had been trampled over by not necessarily adept feet. Such a rejection, however, he was accustomed to, even at this early stage in his career, and it was moreover of a sort which new work often receives from the established servants of the current fashion. The guardians of fashion will always be repelled by the styles of new work going forward, and their repugnance will be fuelled by the subconscious dread that such new styles might oust the ones currently accepted.

Yet O'Ryan fumed. He would get these Cruze-Antonios and Snares! He would flay their simpering, moribund, sluglike limbs! No work was perfect! What did they expect? Shakespeare himself had extremes of oddity in his use of language. But these modern styles, these flabby puddings of prose, with their nervelessness and lifelessness and lack of rhythm and spirit: O'Ryan would expose them! He would reveal to the world their languid, effete pansy-language, and corruscate them with massive polemics! It was only the force of faded fashion that sustained these flatulent slugs. There was no real enthusiasm for them among the public. It was only the subsidised art-moguls, and the BBC, and the trendy reviewers, who were taken in by these pusillanimous prissy-mouthed mimblers! Flabby and feeble in themselves, the trendies of the establishment could not recognise the blatantly geriatric state of these styles. But once O'Ryan had attacked these blithering, senile, weedy supurations, and once his own work had changed the fashions towards vigour, strength and inspiration, then the old styles would merely excite a vengeful scorn!

As O'Ryan sighed forcefully at the thought of the Snare-slugs being torn to pieces by their long-oppressed subjects, his attention gradually returned to the second letter. But then a procession arrived through the lodge behind him, and put thought of letters briefly out of his mind. The pageant was a strange one: pair on pair of little boys, dressed in black academic gowns and wearing tiny academic mortar-board caps, bounced untidily from the road outside into the college grounds and snaked forward along the path O'Ryan had taken. Turning to their right they then filed in through the perpendicular Gothic arch leading to the cloisters, and soon were heard disappearing with echoing footsteps into the gloom that led to the college chapel. O'Ryan chuckled at the merry sight of those who provided a misty May Day world with a clutch of spring carols.

As he watched this procession, behind him loomed darkly the ancient stones of Grammar Hall. This edifice, now used for undergraduate rooms, was the most ancient building of the college, a hall built for the original Grammar School, and which formed the basis for the college to grow around. The Grammar School in effect still survived, but had moved over on the other side of the river, and bore the name of St Mary's College School. It was this school that supplied the little jogging row of choir-boys, who like midget dons, had clattered their way into the chapel. Theirs were the voices that soon would be hooting the ancient antiphons of vespers. O'Ryan seemed to be surrounded behind, in front and in his hands with questions of grammar. The significance of these processions and sights grew, when O'Ryan turned to the second letter.

Dear Mr O'Ryan,
I was delighted to hear from the President that we are to take tutorials together. From all he has said about you, I am already inclined to you, sensing as I do a brother in feeling. I understand we are to meet at eleven on Tuesdays. and that you have an essay question already. However, I must ask you to change the venue from the one which has

been arranged. You may not know this, but I have an invalid daughter, considerably younger than myself, whom I am occasionally to be seen wheeling about in an antique Bathchair around Oxford. She has tragically become rather iller of late, and this next Tuesday I can see that I won't like to leave her. Could you come to my house? The address as you see is Number Eleven Foxview Road, Boar's Hill. It is an old house, and I am somewhat deaf, so let yourself in, and if no one appears wait in the study for me, even though it may seem I am not coming. Looking forward to meeting him whom I sense will be a lifelong friend,

Yours sincerely,

E. Alting

To O'Ryan still fretting from the ignorant insults of the first letter, this second letter came as a joyful thunderclap. He could not believe it! It was too amazing! Too glorious! Too uncanny! Too perfectly and goldenly fated! O'Ryan let out a worshipping sigh of extreme relief, joy and safety. He felt a heavenly path had opened up before him: a firm, measured, masculine way; a promising, fated optimistic way; a way into a grand and unified future. His mind's eye indeed pictured a road set among cypresses and umbrella pines, closed about by dignified monuments with Roman lettering, coaxing his footsteps towards a buoyant, rich landscape of vineyards, idyllic farms, Renaissance hunting lodges and dome-inspired cities.

For the plain facts could not be doubted: the letter had come from the old man in the garden! It was from the very old man whom O'Ryan had been searching so fruitlessly for so many days: he was none other than his new literature tutor. Not only that but the other plain fact was that the girl — the girl in the Bathchair, with the sublime and dreamingly beautiful face, with whom O'Ryan had fallen hopelessly in love, and for whom also he had been even more desperately searching for the last few days — she was the daughter of the man who had been appointed his tutor! And the final plain fact, or at least strong possibility was — to judge from the tone of the letter — that the old man in the garden, who was his new literature tutor, and whom he would be meeting the day after tomorrow, was of such a mind and so generous and uninhibited in his feelings, that O'Ryan might well have occasion at that sublime and much-anticipated meeting which was now far less that even forty-eight hours away, to meet the girl in the Bathchair!

It was everything he could have wished for! It was the solution to absolutely all of his troubles! It was the perfect remedy for the difficulties he had had with the English Faculty in Oxford and the impossibility of finding any one who actually knew what literature was. It was the provision of a friend and a confidant with whom O'Ryan could discuss all these vexing literary matters which plagued his consciousness but about which — due to the blindness of fashion — it was impossible to talk to anyone alive — with the result that like Machiavelli and other spurned geniuses before him he had to make do with conversation with the dead! And finally and most ecstatically it was the sublime promise of a meeting with the girl who for him was the embodiment of the chatelaines of the troubadours, the Virgin Marys of the Cistercian mystics and the idols of the practitioners of the *dolce stil nuovo*, the love of whom lit the whole lives of their canzonierists to such a degree that they, the worshipper and the worship all became One!

Having ecstatically thrown thanks up to the clouds, O'Ryan buried his head in the letter and read it all over again. And then again. Phrases from it rang in his head like splendid continental bells summoning folk to mass in harmonised booms through steep, laundry-draped backstreets. 'Sensing as I do a brother in feeling'! What a phrase! What sentiments! And how miraculously perceptive of Dr Alting to sense so much so soon — and yet how just! They *were* brothers, undoubtedly, O'Ryan had felt that too! Right from the first moment he had felt they were brothers! — in spite of the fact that their mother would have had to have produced her second offspring at somewhere around the age of 82!

'Him whom I sense would be a lifelong friend'! Yes, that too! How full-hearted it was! How unlike the frigid formality behind Snare's supposed slanginess and sex-jokes! How firm and supportive! And how just! This was what O'Ryan had sensed himself as soon as he saw Dr Alting. They were to be friends, and life-long friends at that. Together they would go through the hurdles and . . . O'Ryan had a sense of proportion which occasionally suspended the wildness of his imagination, and once he noted his reason calculating Dr Alting's age yet again, he had the wit to see that a lifelong friendship with an eighty-year-old man could not hope to be in the Oliver-and-Roland class. But not be be outdone, O'Ryan immediately seized on the poignancy of the situation to sigh with emotion.

But then he had another thought: Dr Alting must be enlisted in O'Ryan's great crusade! O'Ryan must tell the old man all his thoughts about the futility of modern literature and get him to help him overthrow the lot! The novel they must tackle first. The novel must be obliterated! Both the modern novel and that of the Romantic Realist! He felt sure that his tutor would share his view of the modernists, and think that their wretched movement should be liquidated. But also the novels of the Romantic Realists who still dragged on their slow length from the Nineteenth Century: these should be swept away also! Why write any further these cloying, pathetic, basically feminine fictions? Were there no men to write romances or epics? O'Ryan hated the novel's delicate, womanly narrative form, the leisureliness, and the soft-focused, motherly, heavy-breathing female indulgence. The idea of following one drooled-over character through a whole book as though the sun shone out of his ass, and incessantly stopping all the action to go into his head, and examine his every thought and impulse: this was the way women wrote! You would never catch O'Ryan mapping the mental bowel-movements of his heroes!

But then he had another thought: he himself was a poet! Poetry was the prize they were after. Dr Alting with his great experience must help him launch his poetic career. So far he had never managed to get a poem printed anywhere. Dr Alting with his literary contacts, his taste, his foresight and his vision, could set O'Ryan forward on the road towards public acclaim: vanquisher of the novel, reviver of the classics, reformer of poetry! O'Ryan must send Dr Alting a bundle of his poems at once so that he can read them before they meet. It was good that a tutor should have some idea of the abilities of a student before he attempted to teach him. Yes, he would get them ready tonight and post them tomorrow morning. Dr Alting would have one day to read them before they met. He could even read the wonderful love-poems O'Ryan now wrote, inspired as he was by Dr Alting's daughter!

'Good new is it, O'Ryan?' said Fosdyke.

O'Ryan looked up from his reverie. Having arrived in the

twilight-filled cloisters he took his eyes off the typewritten letter with both wonder and concentration.

'Er — well, it is as a matter of fact. The second letter anyway,' he said at last.

'That's grand!' said Fosdyke.

Bergson was hovering in the background, and Fosdyke turned round to him and some others. 'O'Ryan's had a bit of good news,' he said cheerily. 'Grand, isn't it? After all the trouble he's been in.'

'Very pleased to hear it, Nigel,' said Bergson coming up soberly.

O'Ryan looked up, clear-faced and sighed. 'Hello, O ye chaps. I'm sorry I haven't been around much of late. I've been a bit preoccupied, and haven't had the zest to come in the pub. It's been strange. But maybe things are on the mend.'

'Ah well,' said Fosdyke, 'we understand, Nig. You're in love after all: we appreciate that. It's not a letter from her, is it?'

'No, no. It couldn't be. She doesn't even know my name.' frowned O'Ryan, with his heart beating excitedly none the less at the thought. 'But it may well be something to do with that. I can't be sure — in fact, I don't really dare even to hope, but it may — I . . . just . . . may be about to get in touch with that —' a big sigh followed, 'that girl I told you about the other day.'

'Well then, that is magnificent!' Fosdyke turned round to where the rest of the gang were hovering just by the archway on the New Buildings side. 'O'Ryan may get to home base soon!' said Fosdyke chirpily.

The others leered.

'Oh, come off it!' O'Ryan laughed blushingly. 'It's not like that at all,' he heaved a great sigh again. 'All the same,' he waved the letter up and down, 'you can't know what a relief it is for me to get this letter. I've been half crazy of late I must admit, but somehow this has cleared the matter up completely!'

'We all share in your delight, Nigel,' said Bergson with incredible portentousness.

O'Ryan was smiling and shaking his head from side to side. 'I think I better go and cool off in the gardens. I really can't get over this. If you're dining in, see you at dinner.'

O'Ryan hesitantly floated his way out through the little archway and off into the twilit college garden.

Just as he passed beyond ear-shot of the arch, a hideous snorting as if from a whole herd of cattle exploded in the cloisters, and a group of shadowy figures reeled and collapsed about the Gothic arches — one actually falling backwards over the sill onto the lawn — in painfully suppressed hysteria. While the born poet strolled, taking a clearer view of the autumn, at ease in the amber of the sunset, his friends rolled about holding their stomachs and rasping their palates in a Medieval carnival of shades.

Chapter Four

'A return to cold, spiritless Classicism is the last thing we want.' said Tenderson. 'If we agree to the Hargreaves design for the quad we will be giving a signal to the whole country that Oxford is starting to march with the theme-park Revivalists. It's bad enough having that awful Oxford Story side-show luring people into its maw with grotesque waxwork figures! If we actually start building the phoney pastiches on the streets as well, then we really will be throwing in the towel! Are we to admit that we have no ideas of our own, that our age is irrelevant, that among Oxford buildings we have nothing to show for *our* century? You may want to make Oxford even more of an extension of the London tourist-trap, but *I* don't. I think of it as a living modern city, and I believe we must vote for the quad-design that states this loud and clear!'

The Estates Committee meeting was in full swing. Around the large, mahogany table of the SCR conference room the fellows of St Mary's College sat in late afternoon debate. While the Estates Bursar, Dr Fobey stared manically at the wall, nervously reining himself in like a hysterical race-horse; while Sir Walter Lawrence pondered thoughtfully over his pen as he slowly tapped it first one way then the other way on the table, and while Dr Werble hesitated as to whether to speak at all, the rest of the dons were shuffling and butting in on one another energetically.

'May I take issue with Dr Tenderson's judgement of modern Classicism?' said Harold Revere. 'I don't think anyone would attempt to call the Classicism of Quentin Hargreaves cold and spiritless. I think most people would agree that his riverside development at Greenwich, and his houses in Richmond Park are examples of a Classicism which is lit with airiness and fancy. And I would maintain that it is completely unnecessary to castigate Hargreaves's work in order for us to reject it as a design, just as it is completely unnecessary to repudiate the trends of modernism in order to reject Hammerstein's plans. Modernism has its place. The most ardent supporter of the Prince of Wales and the most rampant Classicist would agree with that. No one is ever suggesting that you try to build skyscrapers on strict Classical conventions, but —'

'What about that ghastly broken-pedimented thing in New York?' said Tenderson.

'That's just a Postmodernist joke,' said Revere. 'There's a great difference between larky pastiches of bits of Classicism, or classical ornament stuck jokily onto otherwise modern buildings, and the true Classicism of Quentin Hargreaves!'

'I think I'd rather have the pastiche, all in all,' said a don.

'But look at Hargreaves's design!' said Revere. He gestured down to the model for the quad which had a colonade and a cupola embellishing a traditionally proportioned façade, a rusticated archway leading out onto Long Wall Street and a small pavilion type of penthouse overlooking the deer-park. 'You can't have a more happy building than that! Do you think either the building or the people are happy in that monstrosity over the river, where undergraduates are cooked in an oval slate-shingled prison specially constructed to magnify all noise and inconvenience?'

'The President hasn't put his view yet, I notice,' said Fobey staring at him manically.

'Well,' said the President after a pause, 'as you all know, I have declared an interest in this. Quentin Hargreaves is a friend of mine, as I have said, and I have dealt with his firm. It might be rather unethical for me to attempt to cast a vote on the matter. But I must admit I am definitely in favour of a building retaining the character of its surroundings and I do feel that in the countless number of unfortunate places where this has not been done in Oxford, the results are both depressing and degrading. I think we have all heaved sighs at the sight of the soon-out-of-fashion modernist oddities of Oxford. But I really shouldn't say even that.'

Fobey glared at the President, then said 'Well, I think we have all said our say. Perhaps we should move on. I might just add that as far as my own position is concerned, I don't see how I can continue in the post of Estates Bursar if my advice is over-ruled on this matter. I seem to remember we were all most complimentary to Oscar Hammerstein when he came to the guest-night. I think it would be the grossest of discourtesies to reject his design now. As we know, we shall vote on this at the next meeting, and as the President has told us, we have been offered his apologies in advance. Sir Walter is indeed away all next week.'

'Yes, I shall be in London unfortunately,' said Sir Walter. 'I shall stay on after delivering the Demison Lecture for the conference at the Foreign Office. But for the reasons I have stated, I don't feel I can honourably vote on this matter. And as a balance to the point I have just made I would say this. I don't think it is any good us going ahead with the Hargreaves plan unless quite a strong majority of us are convinced it is right. I think if the matter was forced in a direction of what is — after all — a fairly new departure for an Oxford college, then the matter might stir up controversy which in the end would cause people to take sides. I don't see that this is best presented as a fighting matter. I would like to think that we all respect our heritage, and that none of us wishes to damage it. But it does seem the more usual course to go for the modern extension. Startling and obtrusive though this particular design may be, its acceptance would none the less be falling in with general practice. So I would ask you all the think the matter over most seriously before you reach your decision next week, and not vote for Hargreaves unless you are certain and prepared to defend your stance thereafter. I don't want this to become a source of controversy in the SCR. As you know, I am a great believer in people getting on with one another, and I consider it most inefficient to conduct ceaseless political feuds.'

'Thank you, President,' said Fobey. 'I think that could be said to clinch the matter, since on the last count we were considerably more in favour of Hammerstein than Hargreaves. I trust that view will continue next week. I haven't of course myself actually told Hammerstein this in so many words, but I must tell you all that at the guest-night he did most definitely gather the impression that the majority of the committee favoured his plan. Now, I think that concludes the business.'

'Perhaps not,' said Revere. 'There's still the question of the Maeonides's mansion. If we were not able to discuss it in matters arising from the minutes, could we not discuss it now? I can't see why for the last two meetings we have been told that the matter is not yet ready for discussion.'

'Well,' said Fobey quickly, 'if you remember the week before last Dr Werble preferred to leave the matter until he had researched it a little more deeply, and this week I am to tell you that I have taken the whole question over myself. I'd rather not discuss it at this juncture, but I hope next week to give you some definite news of action taken. Hopefully that we have a house agent and a price set for the sale.'

The President interjected. 'I should also mention that I have told Dr Fobey that a factor we perhaps all ought to bear in mind here is that there does seem to be a renewed interest in Maeonides. I appreciate that the decision about the house was taken before I myself took up my position here, and it would not be seemly for me to seek to alter that. On the other hand I have told Dr Fobey that only the other day I received a letter from a television company expressing an interest in filming in the house and in using it to give an authentic background to an outline of Maeonides's work and beliefs. We need not necessarily conclude that growing interest such as this should mean that we now rethink the decision to sell. But we could at least make it a condition of sale or an entailment that the house is maintained as a place of interest for followers of Maeonides.'

'Sir Walter,' said Tenderson long sufferingly. 'Maeonides has no followers. We discovered that all too well when we looked at the matter before. Quite honestly, I think his scholarship and the absurd width of his interests preclude him from ever being one of those figures who make a startling come-back. Those sort of frantic disciplinarean beliefs of his have been entirely discredited. Quite honestly, we all agreed that it was a positive embarrassment to the college to acknowledge his membership of the Senior

Common Room. We all felt without exception that we should sever the link. I think most of us would advise that the request from the television company is firmly rejected.'

Sir Walter raised his eyebrows noncommittally.

'I think the matter may well be settled before next week,' said Fobey quickly. 'Perhaps we could now consider the meeting closed.'

Fobey got up briskly, gathered his papers about him, and walked out the door before anyone could detain him further.

*   *   *   *

When Fobey came to the college entrance, the Head Porter, Albert Lodge, suitably attired in dark jacket and bowler hat, came out of the office, and greeted him. 'Ah, Dr Fobey, here we are then!'

'The meeting ran rather late, I'm afraid, Lodge,' said Fobey. 'But if you're prepared, we could leave straight away.'

'Just a minute, sir, if you don't mind,' said Lodge, and with a purposeful stalk he went back into the college towards Grammar Hall and called after an undergraduate who was loitering, kicking pebbles over the lawn, with a few pals. 'Mr McDowell!' he called. 'Mr McDowell, could you come 'ere a minute?'

Mr McDowell duly shuffled up.

Lodge stood four-square with his bowler hat levelled commandingly, as McDowell muttered 'Yo?' and scooped back the pair of lolling locks which he sported on either side of his central parting.

Lodge held up his finger, then turned and nodded for Fobey to come over.

'This is Dr Fobey, as you probably know,' said Lodge. 'Tell 'im what you told me about what you saw a couple of weeks ago. Don't spare the details. Dr Fobey's not going to be shocked if you 'ave to admit you were sloshed out of your mind when it happened.'

'Oh, yo!' laughed McDowell. 'I was a bit merry. But I really did see it. I mean, I remember at the time thinking: McDowell, you're drunk, now hold on there. But I took a really good look at it.'

'Where is all this leading?' said Fobey irritably.

'I think what Mr McDowell is trying to tell you in 'is leisurely way', said Lodge 'is that he was proceeding into the cloisters at 'alf past one in the morning, when he saw a ghost.'

'What sort of a ghost?' interjected Fobey with extreme nervousness.

McDowell lolled his head forward, chuckled, sneered, scooped his hair back, and muttered, 'Well, yo, that's just what it was, actually. A ghost. Lodge put it like it is. Yo, yo. I mean —' he frowned thoughtfully and looked serious, 'I was feeling pretty awful, and I turned into the cloisters, and I saw this woman waving at me —'

'Woman!' jumped Fobey. 'Was this a Victorian woman with two pistols?'

'Oh God, no!' snorted McDowell. 'I mean, when I say woman, I'm only going on her wearing a dress, or long robes or whatever. I didn't actually see a woman's face.'

'Why not?'

'Well, she was wearing — like — a mask.'

'A terrible, tall, horned mask with its mouth open in a great scream?' said Fobey with desperate resignation.

McDowell looked at him for some time, then bit his lip and with his eyes flickering round said, 'Well, no, actually. I mean, she had a mask but — well, it was a pretty funny sort of mask, and a kind of half-mask too: didn't cover her chin. And I mean it had — well, a giant hooter, to put it bluntly. You know, a really, really, seriously great conk: huge nose, sticking out. Rather comic really. And the woman sort of looped and goose-stepped around —'

'Goose-stepped!' blurted Fobey.

'Well, a kind of chicken-walk.' McDowell roughly prodded his legs forward with toes pointing, and lurched his chin back and forth. 'And she was sort of staring up towards the tower or over the way to the river or the Botanical Gardens and kind of beckoning.'

'Beckoning?'

'Beckoning,' McDowell nodded sagely, 'calling people in.'

Fobey stared. 'And did they come?'

'Well, no, that was it actually.' McDowell shrugged and stared at the ground. 'I was feeling pretty sick by this point, and I might have just moved aside slightly to vomit. I cleared it up, though. Honestly. As much as I was able. But I did feel bloody queasy. All the next day too. I didn't think anything of it, really. I only told Lodge as a bit of a joke. He likes to keep a check on the college ghosts, don't you, Lodge?'

'I like to keep a check on everybody, Mr McDowell, whether of earthly or spiritual manifestation.'

* * * *

'And have you heard of this figure before, Lodge?'

'Yes, Dr Fobey, I have,' said Lodge, as they drove together over Folly Bridge, and began the long, bicycle-dodging trek down the Abingdon Road.

'The figure of a loping, large-nosed female figure, madly probing about and beckoning has been seen before on many separate occasions.'

'For how long?'

'Oh, years!'

'Since before we last considered the Maeonides's house?'

'I can't exactly say,' frowned Lodge. 'But I have the feeling that this one is an old ghost. I think she's been around since olden times. I don't think she's ever really been lost.'

'Lost?' Fobey wrinkled his lip. 'Lost? Can you *lose* a ghost?'

'Oh, yes sir,' Lodge turned his lips down at the edges and nodded. 'Oh yes, yes. The spirit goes out of things, you see. And when it's lost, it's lost.'

Fobey looked hurriedly over to the fields that led down to the river. The evening was all about them, and the mists were rising from the Isis and creeping towards the houses that clustered on the far side of the road. Down on the river, boat-house and lock were already dank with the seeping obscurity, and a solitary pony with knotty tail was quietly vanishing in the fog, as its own breath steamed before it among the willows.

'We must talk about the Maeonides house,' said Dr Fobey. 'You were part of both the previous attempts to sell it and clear it out?'

He darted a look at Lodge, who nodded.

'And did you see the manifestations yourself?'

'Most of 'em,' said Lodge.

'And —?'

'I wouldn't say all of 'em.'

'And what did you see?'

Lodge paused and then let out a long sigh. 'Ghosts, you see, Dr Fobey, are spirits. They have a life like everyone else, but they are a lot more secret than everyone else. They don't really like being disturbed. But some of the scouts and the dons too saw small ghosts and big ghosts, outside and in, and the Greek ladies were about too, because, you see, Professor Maeonides was a Professor of Greek. A Regius Professor too.'

'*Greek* ladies?' said Fobey incisively, as he dodged into the roaring traffic about the Abingdon Roundabout and swerved over towards the dual carriageway. 'Why do you call them Greek ladies?'

'Well, that's what they are. I reckon there could be anything up to nine ghosts, and the nine of them are the spirits of Maeonides's nine daughters, and they show 'emselves in the manner as 'ow 'e named them as the Nine Muses of ancient times. Now Dr Werble saw a lady in Victorian dress with two pistols, but that's only because, being a modern person, 'e can't see back beyond a hundred years or so. 'E sees 'is version of what 'is consideration tells him is the spirit of tragedy. But most ordinary people see a proper Greek Muse in long robes, boots on stilts and a proper Greek mask. Because one of Maeonides's daughters was called after the spirit of tragedy. And the spirit of tragedy is called Melpemone.'

'Well, of course, I'm quite aware of that,' said Fobey, and then went silent.

Lodge tilted his bowler hat, folded his arms and sat back in his seat.

The car now swerved round the second roundabout, and headed up the road towards Boar's Hill. Fobey switched on the headlights, as the overhanging trees made the road black and menacing. The driveways of grand houses loomed up on his left, and behind him reflected in the mirror jumped and jolted the picture of Oxford spires sinking into the gloom of dusk. Headlights of cars came glaring towards him, and shot past plummeting down the hill. They crossed into Foxview Road, found the drive, and came upon Number Eleven as it was outlined with its tall gables against the dying sky.

When they had halted in the drive, Fobey switched off the

engine and turned to Lodge urgently. 'Do you seriously expect me
to believe, Lodge, that this ghost that has shown itself to the estate
agent and to Dr Werble in two different guises is really the Muse
of Tragedy?'

Lodge shook his head. 'No, sir. The ghost is the ghost of the
professor's daughter, Melpemone. But she shows herself as the
spirit of tragedy. The professor has a lot of ancient books up in
that house, and his daughters — only a few of 'em married —
were very learned girls. And they all specialised in the types of art
as the professor had given 'em names for. They liked it that way.
And they live on in that way. And they like their life secret, quiet,
forgotten, neglected. If you're thinking of shaking 'em out of this
house, Dr Fobey, you better be prepared for the consequences!'

'What do you mean by that?' Dr Fobey was startled.

'Well, sir, I think you're thinking of doing away with this place,
in spite of all the trouble the college has had over it before. I
reckon you're come up 'ere expecting to 'ave a look around, make
sure it's full of saleable items, and then 'ave some auctioneer come
and 'aul the lot off.'

'Sh!' Fobey looked startled at the house, as though afraid it
might be listening. 'Lodge, I'd be grateful if you'd keep your
theories to yourself. The college has a duty to preserve the
memory of its great scholars of the past, and I hope to be able to
salvage some such memorial for the professor out of this. But
money is money, Lodge, and the college can't throw away funds
for the sake of sustaining a few fantasies!'

Lodge lifted his eyebrows. Dr Fobey lurched over to the back
seat, dragged up a briefcase, and then hurled himself out of the
car in a surge of indignation. 'The sooner we stop all this nonsense
the better!' he muttered as he slammed the door. Not looking at
the house, he fumbled in his pockets, drew out the key and strode
up towards the porch.

Lodge quietly got out of the car and looked up at the tall roof
with relish.

Fobey attacked the lock. He jammed the key in. He forced it
round. He heaved the door open and darted inside. He undid his
briefcase and with hurrying hands pulled out a plan of the house
and an inventory. He put the briefcase down on a chair by the
mirror, and looked about him purposefully.

By the time Lodge had entered the house, and was standing on the doormat gazing into it and looking round with thoughtful eyes, Fobey was in the parlour darting his gaze around the oil-painting of the Scottish bull, the pot-pourri, the table, the chairs, the cupboard. He saw a bookcase in an alcove and rushed up and looked at it. Then he strode out again and went down the hall towards the study.

Since the conservatory caught his eye, he leant into it to peer about, then he lurched back to consult the plan to see if it were marked. Having ascertained that it was, he found another book-case along the passage and peered at it with difficulty. He lit his cigarette lighter.

'Ah, Tscharlgrüber,' he murmured, 'Tillyard, Freytag, Polti: all books not in the Bodleian.'

He lifted his eyebrows eagerly, clicked out the lighter. Then his eye was caught by the drawing room opposite. He peered into that, saw that it had no bookcases, then looked down hurriedly at the inventory.

'Where's the kitchen?' he said suddenly.

'Through 'ere, sir,' said Lodge still standing by the door, pointing back to a region on the dark underside of the staircase.

But Fobey's eye had now travelled up the staircase, and drawing in his breath, he at once bounded up the steps two at a time.

Lodge strolled through the old house, looking about reminiscently. He went right of the front door, and passed down a very dark corridor that led by the dining room towards a whole suite of rooms connected with the kitchen. It was dark, so he switched on the light, and the electricity at once lit up a spacious, terracotta-tiled kitchen with a large scrubbed table in the centre, about which eight, nine or even ten people could sit. Dust was over everything, and some leaves had blown in from a broken window in the pantry, but the room retained a homely feel, with its china set along the mantlepiece, and its huge Welsh dresser stacked with blue-and-white willow-pattern plates, whose ultramarine patterns just managed to glow through the dust. Lodge walked over to the sink and tried the tap. The house clanked with the water-pressure in the pipes, and a spew of rust-coloured water spat out and splashed up from the sink.

Lodge stopped. He thought he heard something. He went out of the kitchen, and walked down the hall to the foot of the stairs.

'Are you all right, Dr Fobey?' he called.

'What?' came an angry but muffled shout.

Lodge left it at that.

Looking out briefly at the sunset over the garden, Lodge gazed up the stairs and then down at the study door on his left. Quietly he went up to it and turned the knob. It stuck a bit, but eventually yielded. Lodge creaked the door open, looked in and chuckled with delight. Then he entered and shut the door behind him.

Upstairs meanwhile Fobey was prying about busily, hunting among the many bookcases that were dotted here and there in dusty passages. His flickering lighter kept switching on and off, and he would crouch down and dart up with enthusiasm.

When he stood back in the middle of the landing, he counted off the bedrooms he had checked, to see if there were really ten, as stated in the prospectus. But he only counted five. Sombrely his gaze turned to the second staircase, as he realised he would need to check up on the second floor.

Yet something in him was slowing down. Something was getting nervous. Something was reluctant to go any further into a dark, deserted house, where anything could be lurking, menacing in the more and more remote rooms. But then he shook himself and making as much noise as he could busily started up the second flight.

But suddenly he stopped. With a start he turned round and over his shoulder stared out of the window which overlooked his ascent. He could swear he saw out of the corner of his eye a face staring in at him. It was on the Oxford side, and as he peered hard at the bouncing boughs of the tree which rustled in the wind outside, he managed to convince himself there was no face there. So shiveringly he turned his back on the window, and though he felt the face at once return, continued up the dusty carpet. A thrill of horror crept up his back and over his neck, as he climbed on up the stairs, and he hunched his shoulders as if to get them out of reach.

Then Fobey stopped completely. His legs were afraid now. First his shoulders and neck, and now his legs. This was absurd! He could not behave like a child! Yet he hesitated about carrying on up the stairs. He felt as if little spidery hands might be soon grabbing at his ankles. The dark above him seem to hang over the staircase like a black region of terror into which he was intent on thrusting his head. His resolution was fading too. Did he need to check the top storey? There would be no books up there surely. He dithered, but then forced himself to lurch up onto the landing.

All about him in the gloom hung the doors of many bedrooms, each one maliciously waiting for him to enter. What could be in those rooms? What had been lurking there, hiding there for so many years? He couldn't even see a yard in front of him, and the darkness seemed to want to fold him in its embrace of horror. There was a window at the end of the landing. Fobey needed to see light. He needed to look at daylight again, or the relic of it, or a scene beyond the house.

With a spurt of purposefulness, determined to master his fear, he stalked over towards the window and grasped its sill. The sill felt wet and clammy, and as he looked out onto the woods and garden, he saw dwarves crawling towards the house. He shut his eyes. He was worried about his mind. There was something wrong with him. He could not have seen what he saw. He thought he saw dwarves because he had heard tales of them before. Yet even so, when he looked again, the bushes and plants, the hedges and trees that nodded in the wind were dwarves writhing towards the house. A sea of dwarves was thrashing and crawling over the landscape, clawing their way up the slope, ready to attack the castle on the hill and to tear the house and its inhabitants apart.

He must get out of the house, he decided. Or he would make a fool of himself. He had heard so many ridiculous tales from so many gullible people, that the alarming details were just rioting in his imagination. So he must go down and find Lodge and drive back to the college. Lodge was a reassuring character for all his blunt obtuseness, and once he saw him again, things would be better. He had seen enough anyway to know that his plan was right. He need not search the house any more. So he must just get out.

Fobey found, while so furiously thinking, that he had walked back along the shadowy landing, and was trapped in the far side, surrounded by doors. Aghast he looked back at the window he had just left. Now he was imagining dwarves crawling up to the window-ledge, their hands reaching up, their heads bobbing, their eyes greedy, ready to invade the floor and trap him there up high in the building. He sighed with exasperation and fear. He did not seem able to control his own mind. It was as if something were taking it over.

Marshalling his courage, Fobey walked back towards the head of the stairs, and with his knees careering out unsteadily on either side, wobbled his way down them again. But his ankles and feet felt numb, and fear had made all his limbs blundering and lazy. He tripped, saved himself from tumbling, and held out his hand to the bannister to steady himself, then snatched it back fearfully without any reason. He took a last step onto the floor. Then he looked up.

He saw the face at the window, which seemed to be on a body at least thirty foot high once again. Yet it must be — he told himself — the way the trees move in the wind, and this accounted for its writhing expression, its weird shifting cheeks and sneering lips like an idiot. Then Fobey could swear he saw the face draw back from the window, in order to shove a hand through the glass to grab him.

Fobey once more controlled himself. He only had one more flight to go now, and he was on the ground again. He had only to move along the landing to the other staircase and then his descent of that would bring him onto the ground floor and safety. Yet somehow he could not get himself to move forward. Somehow he feared to tackle any more steps. What's more he sensed there was something behind him on the stairs he had just descended. He swung round.

Well, how remarkable! With a sudden sense of normality, he saw an amazing sight. There was Lodge sitting on the stairs with his legs apart and his hands knitted together. He must have been waiting for him all the time! That's why he must have sensed there was somebody there.

Lodge was sitting in a remarkably calm fashion, hunched forward, with his head bent down, so that only the top of his bowler hat showed itself to Fobey. Fobey's exclamation must have attracted Lodge's attention, for now the bowler hat started to rise.

Just as the brim rose above eye-level, it revealed what lay underneath. Lodge's broad, calm, eminently normal face looked at Fobey and gave him a smile.

Fobey sighed with relief to see that placid, stolid, self-satisfied grin which he had often noted on people of little intellect. But then he was disturbed to see a look of puzzlement come over Lodge's face, as the head porter looked down at his own ankles.

Fobey gasped with horror as he saw that the rider of the step was missing and merely gave way onto blackness, and jutting out from the blackness two hands were thrust forward to seize on Lodge's ankles. Lodge looked back at Fobey with an expression of horror, and then opened his mouth as if in pain. The hands tugged back at the ankles. Lodge's feet were jerked down into the blackness, then his legs, and his whole torso fell forward.

With a fearful face staring back at Fobey, pleading with hands outstretched, Lodge was then tugged further into the darkness beneath the stairs. His bulging stomach was now wedged in that shallow opening, and yet it was hauled in. Then his shoulders and his elbows held out on either side to prevent him being dragged back: they were also dragged in.

Finally with a brief flash, like the teeth of a dog snapping in the night, Lodge's grimacing face disappeared into the blackness, which — since the underneath of the steps was merely the ceiling of the lower staircase — was a place that in fact did not exist.

Towards Fobey's shaking legs and curled-up toes Lodge's tipped-off bowler hat came bouncing down the carpet, just as up the first staircase came lumbering the hunched, huge shoulders of the masked figure.

*　*　*　*

'I must say you gave me quite a turn when you screamed like that, Dr Fobey,' said Lodge as they got back into the car. 'I never thought of myself as a disturbing figure. I always thought I 'ad a comforting sort of face, but I'm afraid in the dark, you must 'ave taken me for something else.'

Fobey said nothing. He switched on the ignition, revved the engine, put it in gear, and jolted the car into a stall. At once he turned the ignition again, and the car jerked forward on the gear. Fobey looked up at the ceiling, hissed the air through his teeth and controlled himself. Then determinedly he put the gear into neutral, switched on the ignition again, and succeeded in starting and driving the car.

'You know, it was interesting seeing that laurel in the garden sheltered by the long brick wall,' continued Lodge reminiscently. 'I remember going up to the Professor's house soon after I'd joined the college as a very green scout on the kitchen staircase. I was 'elping to deliver some books with one of his girls, Miss Thalia, I think it was — she was a sport, she was! She was married by them, I reckon. But it didn't hold her back. Always careering about. Loved dressing up too! — Anyway, she went outside to see her father, who was an old man by then, but even so 'e was sawing away at this tree like billio! And Miss Melpemone was around at the time — she never got married at all! — and she was wailing away that her dad was going to destroy the whole tree with this ruthless sawing. The tree, you see, 'ad caught the frost really badly. I think it must've been that really bad winter in '47 — Now that's a long time ago! Laurels aren't natural to England in any case — Anyways, the professor turned to her and said "My dear Melpemone —" 'e 'ad a sort of lofty, yet kindly way of speaking, as folk did in those days. You 'ear 'em do it on old newsreels, you know, like of the last war, and there they are wearing their winged collars and such like.

' "My dear Melpemone," he said, "it is very difficult to destroy things in this world. You see that Nature in her infinite wisdom has thought to send a frost sufficient to kill all this wonderful growth of laurel down to its very trunk. But the shrub is not dead. Life exists at a deeper level, and from that life may branches, leaves and flowers again be re-enkindled —" 'e always 'ad a nice turn of phrase, Professor Maeonides — "And so it is in the generations of mankind. Frost and snow destroy the branches of learning and culture, but all is not dead. Life withdraws to the trunk, thence to revive. And even if the trunk itself is stricken, then the roots live on, deep underground, hidden amidst the snows, they conserve their life and the beauty of their florescence, and when time is propititious —" lovely word that: propitious! — "when time is propitious, the shoots will spring again."

' "And my dear Melpemone, my dear, Thalia" — I remember him holding up his finger dictatorial-like, making 'is point, as 'e always did — "even if the whole bay-tree is killed root and branch, all is not lost, for the *form* then survives. The form is like a seed. It can be dried, frozen, blown on the winds, buried a thousand years under the ground, but with a little warmth, moisture, love, it will again grow. The seed-forms hold in them the very formulas of life, just as among your arts, my dears, the types have their eternal shape, and the seed-forms, emerging after their long sleep under the ice of arrogance, ignorance and sloth, need but a little liquor and sunlight and lo! once more the garden is abundant." ' Lodge chuckled to himself. 'I remember 'im gesturing out then to the shrubs as 'e said this, with that quizzical eyebrow of his raised up and that half-grin at the corner of his lips, relishing 'is words: "Lo! once more the garden is abundant!" '

'I have already contacted Jeffersons' the auctioneers in St Michael's Street,' said Fobey, 'they are perfectly willing to take the whole house as a job lot. I shall order a pantechnicon to strip the place and take the contents at once to Jeffersons' store. As to the books, Metabas Moves, a specialist firm of book-removers, have been alerted and will be under instruction to appear at precisely the same moment and load the books. The house I want completely stripped of all its furniture and appointments as soon as possible. And while I am taking these actions, since I believe it will make it easier to sell the property to a developer, as a gesture of goodwill to the Maeonides estate, I shall take the books into the college library. The librarian has agreed to this, the esteemed Mr Strophy, and the books will be stored in the SCR library until their contents can be properly catalogued and assessed. You need not trouble yourself about it any further, Lodge. It is time to kill off this matter for good!'

Lodge knitted his brows and nodded his bowler-hatted head gravely and musically, as they sped off in the darkness towards the lights of Oxford.

Chapter Five

On the Tuesday morning, O'Ryan arose with a sense of sublime anticipation. He shaved humming, he scrubbed his teeth warbling, he washed his face and his person with affectionate and demonstrative jollity. He felt so safe, so cared for, so at home with the situation that was unfolding itself, that he sensed he had become a totally different person from the worried, harried, angst-ridden, haunted O'Ryan of the week before.

One thing he wanted to do in this his first tutorial with Dr Alting was to ask him about the strange dreams he had had just before the day he first saw him in the Botanical Gardens. Somehow O'Ryan just knew he would be able to explain their meaning. In particular he wanted to know about the wailing women, and also the significance of Mozart's Fortieth Symphony, but most of all he wanted to ask him what the giants and dwarves meant. He was sure the dream was leading him towards a great discovery.

The rain was coming down as O'Ryan set off on his bike towards Boar's Hill. He had his essay in his saddlebag: an impassioned appreciation of the beauties of *Othello* both from a dramatic and poetic standpoint, and he draped his raincoat over himself and back over his bag to prevent the paper getting soggy in the downpour. With the drops dashing down his beaming face, exhilarated to be peddling towards what he felt was bound to be an exalted and enlightening encounter, he biked up the slight incline from the drive of his digs, and off onto the Warnborough Road, and up Leckford Road towards the drenched spire of the Church of the Two Apostles.

As he passed onto Woodstock Road, O'Ryan had a strange experience, which brought back for a moment a slight twinge of the fear with which he had greeted the idea that he might be seeing visions. He thought he saw a friend of his, Ramsey, catch a glimpse of the biking born poet and then dart gleefully into a phone-box. He was puzzled by this, as he cycled on past Green College and the Radcliffe Infirmary, but then even more surprisingly he saw outside the restaurant Browns a whole bunch of his comrades cheering and waving at him, as though they wished him well on his exciting new venture. These glimpses were all startling and puzzling — that he had to admit — but could in no respects be thought to be hallucinations.

As O'Ryan pedalled along, he rejoiced to think that he would be able to ask Dr Alting literary as well as phantasmagorical questions. He had posted Dr Alting a sample of his poems, just as he had decided on reading his letter, and included among some of his favourite love-lyrics and Housmanesque ballads on Oxford, he had offered for his gaze some experiments he was making in writing in Classical metres. Apart from wanting to hear what Dr Alting thought of these quantitative experiments, O'Ryan was puzzled to know if there were any tradition for attempting to write this way in English.

The rain had cleared, as O'Ryan hurtled down the hill of St Aldates, past the great gate of Tom Tower and the bastion walls of Christ Church. The Memorial Gardens smelt of wet leaves and the trees gleamed pale beyond the iron gates, leading off into a misty avenue of elms. Past the Police Station he sped, past the new, clean Law Courts, and soon by the the Head of the River pub he was flying the spaces over the Isis. A folly stands in the midst of the bridge, a brick-built tower of a house with niches filled with white statues. The muddy Thames floated below supporting the oars of the colleges, and just as O'Ryan passed, a few Freshers were laughing, having trouble with their strokes, as the rampant little cox bawled at them hoarsely. Oxford smiled after the rain. O'Ryan peddled harder, and set himself up the gradual slope towards the hills.

O'Ryan dreamed then of what would happen when he had finished his tutorial with Dr Alting. When the business was done, he fantasised enthusiastically, and the men had finished their talk, would Dr Alting say: shall we join the ladies? His heart failed, and a sweet, blissful bleeding flowed down towards his middle, as he thought of once more gazing on that angel face. While Dr Alting might for an hour or so engage O'Ryan's mind, there was no doubt where his heart was engaged. Not an hour, but a day, a week, a month, a year he would sit at her feet, till a new autumn's leaves would scatter and cover him up. Of things of the soul he would talk with Miss Alting. He longed also to know her name! He longed to hear her lips quietly speak it! Somehow he knew her voice would be soft, melodious, kind, lulling and close. He spurred his pedals. He pushed his calves exultantly down to the road, a bicycle knight, exultant and instinct with power!

As he zoomed around the car-swirling roundabout and up the steep approach to Boar's Hill, fresh sunlight broke through the towering ashes and beeches to his left. Up sweeping drives the grander houses of Oxford hid their façades, seeking the pine-scented secrecy and silence. Past tufted orchards he made his way, as thrushes sang happily in the brakes, and fields with hay steamed and chesnuts came rattling down. Red berries speckled the autumn hedges, quirky beechnuts lay scattered about the road, red-grey quirrels hopped and twitched on the mossy branches. O'Ryan came to the top of the hill, coasted at last along Foxview Road, and counted the numbers to bring himself to Number Eleven.

With a leap of happiness he found the place and swung straight into the drive. In an overgrown garden and trees festooned with creepers, he saw the decaying house before him. What might have appalled the heart of an older and maturer house-buying person only struck the student as picturesque. The lichen-stained portico, the ivy-covered windows, the moss-dotted roof with slates awry, the desolateness and quietness and untrodden, weedy path were all just features that delighted O'Ryan and seemed to tantalise him with the breath of ancient glories. As one that loved anything old, O'Ryan relished the phantom-house, as though it held the key to the secret of past forms. He set his bike against the ledge of a window that had in it a broken pane, and strode through the seedy grasses up to the door. O'Ryan breathed in a deep breath, set his essay-case firmly under his arm, and seizing the antique bell-knob gave it a hearty pull.

The bell echoed hollowly. It had not rung in that way for many years. It seemed to fright the whole sleepiness of the house. It called back memories of old milkmen with horse and carts, old visitors who had hiked up in plus-fours from Oxford. Edwardian ghosts seemed to be summoned by the muffled ring of a bell that was now still in a cloud of dust. There then began a long period of silence. O'Ryan smiled and sighed. The sun felt soft. It numbed his brain with its warmth. He began himself to feel sleepy. It was for him as if he stood at the moment before a great beginning, at the hour before the curtain rises or battle commences, when all anticipation is run out, and when all preparations are done, and when presence and attention is all that is required. So did O'Ryan feel lulled by that suspended time. And he did not think how long was it since he rang.

But then he considered he must ring again. Dr Alting in his letter had said he was deaf, and so O'Ryan could not find odd the long delay. He pulled out the bell again. The muffled jangle like cow-bells once more went forth over the mountains. And once again the sun stroked him with a leisurely hand, and O'Ryan smiled and rolled up his face towards it. After the autumn shower the sun was almost hot. It seemed to speak of summers long gone. O'Ryan looked back over the garden. It was certainly much neglected. A hedge had grown like a maze to the side of the lawn. A whole flock of sparrows were using it as a vast parliament building, and in the lazy light they cheeped fitfully. Chrysanthemums thrust their confused, flushed faces from beds overgrown with thistles, and Michaelmas daisies dotted the roving bracken with mauve. The colours in the garden held the parched autumn in dalliance, and a kindliness seemed to breed in its fragile staying. Who would want to disturb these weeds that enjoyed the garden's decay, and made a secret banquet of being forgotten?

O'Ryan sighed. Yes, here was a place which Oxford had forgotten, and in neglect there was blessedness. There was no shame or resentment in thus being spurned, for the quietness was watched by a greater presence. He suddenly saw that the things he loved, and which he thought were culpably forgotten, were in fact happy for being left alone. They rejoiced in quiet, in love and consciousness: not to be found in crowds. He came to himself in a secret garden of silence. The forgotten lyric hiding beneath the overhanging brambles, the mighty epic towering alone in the distant glade, the purple deadliness of great tragedy spreading its leaves in the hedgerow: these forgotten blossoms were in bliss. Bliss was the sun that touched their secrecy, and bliss their hidden communion, and bliss was it for O'Ryan to share in it all.

There was a rustling in the house. O'Ryan turned. Seen through the wave-ribbed glass of the window a shape approached to answer the door. It seemed very tall. O'Ryan looked at it puzzled. Was this the Dr Alting he had seen in the garden? But of course not, how could it be? Dr Alting was blind. Somebody else must be answering the door for him. The shape seemed to roll and lope in a strange way. O'Ryan turned aside, looked up at the sky, swivelled on his heel, prepared a face to meet the honoured doctor's embassy.

The door was unlatched, stuck in the jam, was given a heave and shook, shuddering dust in a trailing cloud. O'Ryan was practically laughing at the neglect, but when the door itself slid ajar, behind in the gloom he saw an amazing sight.

'Sumpter!' he gasped in astonishment. 'Sumpter! But can it be you?'

'O'Ryan!' gasped the young man in reply.

'But how can you be here in this place? And anyway, Sumpter, I thought —'

'But the same to you, O'Ryan! What are you doing here?'

'I've come for a tutorial with Dr Alting, the don who lives here. He wrote and asked me to come up to his house.'

'Dr Alting!' said Sumpter in surprise. He pushed his hand through his blond hair, and rubbed it round his designer-stubbled chin. 'But look, come in. Yeah, they said some one was coming. But I'd no idea it would be you. You're pretty wet, you know, O'Ryan. I'll get you a towel. They want you to wait in here anyway. So come on in.'

Sumpter now ushered O'Ryan into the dusty house. The born poet breathed in its quiet air. The sunlight came in at the back and through an amber-stained-glass fanlight fell onto the terra-cotta tiles. A hat-stand stood covered in dust with a homburg hat on it, and some old prints of Oxford were on the walls.

'Just wait in here, while I get it,' said Sumpter showing O'Ryan into the parlour. In this room there was no sun, and things smelt of mould. It had a table in it, which was covered with a large, ginger-coloured cloth of coarse velvet, from which suspended a once-gold fringe. A bowl of what looked like wood-shavings lay on top. It was pot-pourri that had turned white with age. And a weird painting lurched over a sideboard with a lean so severe it had prevented it catching dust: a great horned bull of a Scottish breed looked sourly out at the viewer from a purple-and-amber-heather moor.

As Sumpter went off into the house and along the corridor to the kitchen, O'Ryan shook his head in bafflement. Of all the people to see here in Oxford! Yet perhaps Sumpter was at Oxford! But he never read of this in Dr Arbuthnot's Grammar Academy *Gazette*. On the other hand, he had read other things. It was all very strange — disturbing! O'Ryan frowned. What can have happened?

Sumpter returned now, carrying a towel for O'Ryan, and handed it over to him. 'It's just like old times, seeing you here!' he said. 'Remember the Blond Masai Gang? And the ode you wrote to it? And the javelin competition with those bloody spears?'

O'Ryan took the towel, and chuckled, then sighed as he felt his cold, wet head engulfed in the soft, perfume-smelling warm. Grinning beneath he rubbed his hair, hearing the familiar sound of that forgotten voice and felt as if he was back at home in Africa.

When he took the towel away, he had tousled hair and tears in his eyes, and at Sumpter's laughing face he said, 'Sumpter, what happened? I read in Dr Arbuthnot's *Gazette* that you'd been killed in a car-crash in Nairobi. But damn it, here you are alive! How can I not have heard about it? I've been grieving you all these years. Yet, you bugger, you're damn well not dead after all!'

Sumpter smiled and brushed O'Ryan's hair down. 'I should have got in touch, I know,' he said. 'I'm such a lazy sod, that's my trouble. But in actual fact the report in the *Gazette* was a last minute thing and they got it all wrong. I was pretty badly hurt, but I certainly wasn't dead. There was a correction slip anyway that they put in all the copies. But you obviously had it missing. You're not the only one, O'Ryan. Anyway, I'm here as you see. But listen, I've got to dash off now. What college are you in? I'll get in touch next week, I promise.'

'St Mary's,' said O'Ryan. 'But are you at Oxford?'

'Oh, I'm everywhere. I just can never stay long. You know me! But listen, let's meet and talk soon. St Mary's College: I won't forget. May be we'll all be down there soon. But who would have thought it! O'Ryan!'

'Too true! Sumpter!'

The two looked at each other and smiled.

'It's so strange!' said O'Ryan. 'It's like a time-warp! And you don't look a day older!'

'The blond Masais for ever!' cried Sumpter with a raised fist.

But then O'Ryan heard a shuffling foot in the hall outside, and looked beyond Sumpter down towards the conservatory. He had the feeling of Sumpter sliding away and disappearing down the kitchen corridor, but then he saw an old figure coming towards him.

'Ah Mr O'Ryan,' said a deep, kindly voice. 'That must be you. You've come for your tutorial, I trust. Welcome.' And a white-haired old man approached tapping his cane, and held out his hand for O'Ryan to grasp. The old, dark-spectacled Dr Alting had a shock of white hair which seemed to shoot out at a strange angle from his head. O'Ryan tried to concentrate his thoughts so that he could get a good look at him, but before he could study his face, he was led along the hall into another room.

'You've brought your essay along? Do take a seat.'

O'Ryan found himself ushered into a room in a much better state of repair, which was warm, smelt of firewood, and filled with distant sunlight. Beckoned by the white-haired figure, he sat down on one side of a crackling fire. Dr Alting, though blind, moved around the room with great ease. O'Ryan stared into his face to study it, while the figure sat down in a high-backed leather chair opposite him. O'Ryan wasn't altogether sure that it didn't look rather more like Dr Arbuthnot than anyone else! But perhaps this was just from the shock of seeing Sumpter! What an extraordinary coincidence!

The white-haired ancient felt his way about, put his white cane down within reach, settled some papers on a table next to the chair, then sank back into it with a smile. O'Ryan at last had a chance to stare at the man's face. There was no doubt. He was with the old man in the garden.

'Now I think you have spent four weeks so far this term on the works of Shakespeare?' Dr Alting looked up listeningly. O'Ryan nodded.

But then he realised that nodding was not enough to a blind man. So he grunted a murmur of assent. But since he then thought that even this might not have been heard, 'That is so!' he boomed in confident tones.

'And that you have completed an essay of a general nature on one of the four great mature tragedies, which I have been told is *Othello*?'

Again O'Ryan orated stoutly, as one striving to impress an interview-panel for the post at a Detention Centre. 'That is indeed my first choice.'

There was a pause while Dr Alting felt among some Braille notes on his table.

O'Ryan opened his mouth, sensing his chance to speak, and reluctant to get involved in reading his essay too soon. There was usually a period of time at the beginning of each tutorial — whose object after all was the student's reading of his week's essay — during which pleasantries, weather-comments, sad stories of missing library books or abject excuses could be mutually investigated. But perplexed by the thousand questions he had in his head, O'Ryan had not been able to decide which one to ask first. On the whole he thought that it might be best to break the subject of his own poems. But Dr Alting seemed to have planned to forestall him in any of his hopes, for he at once launched into a bewildering scholarly tirade.

'I should like you to study these,' he said suddenly handing O'Ryan some photocopied papers from the table. O'Ryan stared perplexed at what looked to him like fuel consumption charts.

Dr Alting continued briskly. 'I like all my pupils to master the art of Proportional Synopsis. Proportional Synopsis is a method I have invented for accurately representing the structure of a literary work. You will see from my instructions that it is a means of making a synopsis of a work which is in proportion to the work itself. To construct a piece of proportional synopsis you need to do three things, all of which must be accomplished on one sheet of paper. Mark out a scale of the line numbers or page numbers of a text downwards on a vertical axis, mark the divisions of the work step by step on that scale, and write a synopsis alongside and at pace with these divisions. The result is a summary which accurately reflects the proportions of the text and which plainly reveals its form and content.

'Before you you have both a proportional synopsis of a particular scene in *Othello*, and a proportional synopsis of the play as a whole. Shakespeare's plays habitually have a highly dramatic, central scene in the Third Act which features a crisis and reversal of the plot. Act III Scene iii, the scene analysed, is one of the most dramatic and harrowing scenes of the tragedy, and in it Iago, purely by exciting his jealousy, converts Othello from a noble commander into a bellowing savage. As the proportional synopsis reveals there are two large duologues in this scene which contrast with one another in tone. In the first duologue of 171 lines Othello is tempted originally in a desultorily way and in the most modern sounding, leisurely and naturalistic dialogue. In the second duologue of 161 lines he re-enters already much distressed and out of control, and Iago from that point whips him up into a frenzy. Incidentally as Professor Nevill Coghill has shown, Shakespeare added extra lines towards the end of this scene in order to fill out the measure of the second duologue so as to balance the first, and also to give the end of the scene a grand, poetic and implacable effect.

'In between these two duologues is a bridge passage in which events vital to the plot occur. First Othello has a soliloquy of some 22 lines in which he muses on Iago's honesty. Then Desdemona comes in and there is a 10 line duologue during which she tries to bind Othello's brow with her handkerchief, and having had it rudely brushed from her hand, leaves it on stage as they go out. Emilia enters, picks up the handkerchief and soliloquises for 10 lines on how her husband has begged her to steal it. Then Iago enters and has a duologue of 22 lines with Emilia during which he gets the handkerchief. The proportional synopsis thus shows that by a sequence of balancing sections: 171, 22, 10, 10, 22, 161, Shakespeare has set the crux of Othello's conversion around a central moment, which is at a halfway point of .51 through the whole temptation episode.

'This central moment is, however, also at a halfway point of .53 through the play as a whole, so that the whole play is hung on this tense and decisive moment when the handkerchief, from which

Othello's whole destruction is wrought, quietly flutters to the ground and passes from the good to the evil character. Proportional Synopsis in this particular case reveals a structure of classical poise underlying the tremendous drama of the play. It can also reveal a structure of dynamism, based on the Golden Section, which forces the drama forward with perfect poise. Such supreme artistry — which I freely admit was not consciously counted out by Shakespeare — is merely typical of Shakespeare's works in general, the beauty of whose structures, whether balanced or dynamic, are best revealed by this system of proportional synopsis.'

Dr Alting looked at O'Ryan.

O'Ryan closed his mouth. 'That's amazing!' he gasped at last. 'Do you think Shakespeare planned it like that?'

'You must listen to what I say,' came the reply. 'I have said I do not believe Shakespeare counted the lines with such intent. I consider the result to be the natural product of the beauty and power and detachment of his mind. He did of course plan plays like *Othello* with extreme care. You cannot write that sort of a play without planning its workings like a Swiss watch.'

'May be I could do the same?' said O'Ryan.

'Perhaps you could. Now shall we proceed with your own views on *Othello*?'

But O'Ryan was in a reverie. 'Why haven't I read any of this stuff before?' he said at last. 'This is interesting! This is worth knowing! This really tells you how to write!'

'At the moment it is not of any general interest.'

'But it should be!'

Dr Alting smiled. 'You do not seem to understand the interests of the modern literary world. They are not directed towards such matters as this.'

O'Ryan considered. He was silent for a long time.

Dr Alting smiled at him. 'What was it in particular that made you select the Venetian tragedy?'

O'Ryan sighed. 'Er —' He didn't quite know why Dr Alting put it like that, and also he found it difficult to get his thoughts which had suddenly started floating around pageant-like apparitions in the Botanical Gardens back again on to academic matters. But then he felt inspired. 'Actually,' he said. 'I saw a wonderful traditional-type Russian film of it once that I've always remembered. It just caught that marvellous sadness you get in the Mediterranean twilight. I remember Othello lifting his arms up to the cyclorama which was deep mauve-blue just like the Mediterranean at dusk, as if asking the heavens why did they have to punish him with such extremity just in that place of his heart where they could hurt him most? And all the time we know that he is deluded. There has been no betrayal. How could she betray him? And then I was just reading *Dr Faustus* again, and I thought that with *Othello* we have Shakespeare's version of a fiend dogging a man to get his soul. They have just that same friendly relationship of damnation. But then —' O'Ryan frowned. 'I also became enraged at the way modern critics have spoken about the play. I found Eliot's and Leavis's comments on it simply infuriating. It just seemed so typical of the way modernists can't appreciate Shakespeare. And they were two eminent critics too, not the usual time-serving twitterers.'

'Have you read my late colleague Dame Helen Gardner's lecture on the Noble Moor?' the deep voice was highlighted with a raised quizzical eyebrow cocked above the dark glasses.

'Er — I don't think so, no.'

'She makes the point that *Othello* can be considered a test reaction for the appreciation of the heroic spirit. For the critics who are deficient in responding to the heroic spirit, Othello's last speeches will merely seem to them exasperating, but for those who have sufficiently strong stomachs and can relish the heroic mode in which the greatest literature is written, Othello will seem to be one of Shakespeare's most noble heroes.'

O'Ryan lifted his eyebrows happily. Then he frowned and said, 'Dr Alting, why do critics write such God-awful rubbish?'

Dr Alting gave a little smile. Then he said, 'A Twentieth Century critic spends a great deal of his time trying to interpret literature. The process of interpretation is for him the purpose of reading, and the purpose for which he teaches the work. By interpretation, however, he means translating the work into terms with which the modern world feels comfortable. He is not really interested in understanding the author per se, since this might quite possibly mean him abandoning many if not all of his favourite attitudes, but he wishes to twist the work into a form which gives it a journalistic relevance. The process involves not a change in reader but a change in the text, and in this way he misses the whole educational aspect of literary study.'

'Dr Alting,' said O'Ryan at last, 'before I read my essay, could I ask you something rather strange? I had some weird dreams quite recently, during which I seemed to feel the presence of a mind like yours, and they perplexed me with an anguish I have long suffered. I don't really know if it is me that is sick, or the way I see the world, or the world itself — or at least certain parts of it. And since these parts of it that I find sickening could legitimately be my concern, I feel I must try and settle my mind about them. My dreams were complex, and I saw images like Medieval dream-visions. I met figures and was told things, as Chaucer is in his dream-visions, and I found myself in allegorical places. But there were disturbing things going wrong in them, involving riots and imprisonment and violence. I dreamed of Classical figures or Eighteenth Century people dancing in a ballroom to Mozart's Fortieth Symphony, and then being invaded by dwarves and giants, who brought a whole edifice crashing down. I'm sure you know about my dreams. They seem to me to hold some truth about the modern world which I ought to grasp. This is why I want to ask you about them. What am I to do? Is it me who is mad, or is there something to be discovered?'

Dr Alting stared down at the carpet, his chin sunk into his chest. Then he took off his spectacles and looked at O'Ryan. 'At times in history Fate decrees that a violent discord is struck again and again, the better to spin and impel and enrich and develop the melody. The things which you have seen, Mr O'Ryan, are of the world of violence: the death, destruction and evil of recent centuries. But to seek to understand storms like these is not on the path you have started. Yours is the service of the eternal forms. Put your trust in the deeper things, and serve their disciplines. For look, no clouds can carry off the sun!'

Dr Alting cast his head towards the garden, where the gold lit the apple-boughs, and said, 'Right! Now on with your essay!'

*   *   *   *

From the moments he first spent in Number Eleven Foxview Road, O'Ryan felt he had regained the home-ground. He was no longer a puzzled eccentric, a clown lost in the crush, a soul who had no proper home or profession. He was no longer an outsider, an oddity crated from Africa, a throwback to a peculiar education. He knew he was solitary. Of course he was solitary: he was a man in an alien land. But the land was still a shadow of the true kingdom. Dr Alting had shown him. And somehow he trusted his words warning him of distraction. It was easy to become hypnotised by darkness.

When the tutorial was over, Dr Alting gave O'Ryan work for the following week, and suggested other texts he might read as background. Then he intoned an essay question to which O'Ryan must apply his wits, and which O'Ryan dutifully copied into his notebook. The time was confirmed of their next meeting: Tuesday at Eleven. Then Dr Alting reached over to the table beside him. There were some loose papers on it, and Alting felt them with his hands, seeing which were typed, which were photocopied. He made a selection from them, and held them in his hand, then looked up, ready to speak again to O'Ryan.

'Your poems,' he said, 'were much enjoyed. They have neither the flat, prosey voice of Modernism, nor the trembling excesses of Romanticism. It is possible therefore that they may provide a basis for a return to normal poetry. I have taken the liberty of photocopying them, so as to retain copies, and also of having some of them re-typed. This is because you have attempted to write in quantitative metres, and it was necessary for me to make some corrections. The use in English of quantitative metres is considered by critics to be impossible, and poets like Spenser and Tennyson have failed in such experiments. But Stanyhurst in the Elizabethan era, and in our own Bridges and Ernle, have shown that lines in Classical hexameter can be composed. You are following in this tradition. But you must be strict with yourself. The Classical rules and conventions must be followed.'

Dr Alting hesitated forward to hand them back. O'Ryan was puzzled by the look of them. Then the old man paused and kept hold of them.

'It would be good for you first to pursue your lyric compositions,' he continued. 'You will find that the Classical metres can form a basis for a totally new kind of English verse. And your traditional ballads and love-poems are fresh and inspired. Write them while you are young. But train yourself also in the grander forms. Make a balance in your endeavours between a study of models, a practice of rules, and free inspiration.'

He then handed over the sheaf of papers to O'Ryan, who saw with surprise that not just his poems had been given him. He could not believe it. He looked down at them in a stunned wonder of delight. They were now illustrated by black-and-white drawings. But they were not just illustrations! What he saw before him were the very same patterns and drawings as he had seen in his dreams. He stared back at Alting in wonder. How can this be happening? The old man seemed to sense his amazement.

'Time brings fittingly things together,' he smiled. 'Your poems, those pictures. Together they sign a new integrity. Conjured from the black and white of snow on a winter's night, the machine has printed text and vision. Do not be amazed. It is no marvel. The spirit shapes, and books and words and drawings bring its message. Take them, and when you will, bring more, and make more visions.'

The tutor now shuffled in his chair. O'Ryan took the hint, and got up ready to leave. But a sudden pang overtook him. He was to return to the 'real' world, and a feeling of sadness and loneliness now washed into his heart. A burning question leapt into his brain. The subject had been driven away by intellectual concentration, but it rushed back now into his mind with desperation. Was he to leave the house without any mention of his obsession? Was there to be no sign of Dr Alting's daughter?

The old man put his hand on his shoulder.

'Mr O'Ryan,' he said softly. 'I think I mentioned before I have a daughter. She is an invalid. She lives a lonely life, with me an old man. It is rare for her to have visitors. I wonder if you would care to meet her? If it would not delay you too much, I would think it charitable of you to speak to her.'

O'Ryan tried to control his voice. 'I would love to!' he gasped.

Alting smiled. 'Good. She has her room directly above this. She would also be glad to know if you liked the illustrations to your poems. They are all her own work. She draws always upstairs.'

O'Ryan looked amazed again at the drawings. No wonder he had liked them. 'I love them!' he sighed ecstatically.

Dr Alting spoke on. 'It is sad, but my daughter has chionopathia. It is a disease that saps the strength, and slowly freezes in numbness and neglect. She cannot walk. There are some reports of a cure being developed on the other side of the Atlantic, but we do not allow ourselves to hope too much. Take the drawings up to her, Mr O'Ryan. Her work is never seen. She would like to think it was appreciated.'

'I will,' said O'Ryan.

'Just one more thing,' Dr Alting paused, searching for words. 'I am afraid upstairs,' he said at last, 'you will have to do all the talking. My daughter is dumb. She cannot speak. She lost the use of her voice some years ago, and none have heard her since.'

O'Ryan gasped. Then he shut his mouth. He found tears springing into his eyes.

'The snow takes all away.' Dr Alting sighed. 'But in a world of form and silence, there is beauty and peace. Unheard she is ever happy. And since I know she loves your poems, she is keen to hear *your* voice. Go, but expect not. Sit and see. Nor do not feel you have to speak learnedly. She is no don. And she speaks with her eyes!'

O'Ryan felt the old man now guide him with his kindly hand, and gently lead him back towards the staircase.

There is in all souls a secret staircase that winds in the depths of the mind up to the room which has existed for ever. There by the fire which always burns, in the chairs which always comfort, the heart surrenders and knows its home. The looped-up curtains, safe and close in an eternal childhood, give a view from a constant window always changing — the sun now striking the damson-tree, the shadows on the pond and sundial, the red-stemmed roses casting their petals on the path — yet next to the hearth by the copper coal-bucket and the cold, iron tongs, the muffins of comfort warm before the flames. In a room like this has all come home. In peril or anguish here does the mind return, and everything is well. Towards such a place O'Ryan felt himself now lightly ascend, with his poems in one hand and the drawings in the other.

She was lying lazily in a great French bed in an old-fashioned chamber, where the sunlight caught the gold patterns on the drapes. A cat at the window sat looking out, and did not turn round when he entered. A great mahogany wardrobe leaned into the room. Propped up on pillows in a night-dress of ivory trimmed with effusive lace, under a coverlet of scarlet-and-olive-embroidered lyre-birds, the young Miss Alting, the speechless invalid, sat wanly smiling at O'Ryan: a sight which kicked out the bottom of his soul.

'Hello, Miss Alting,' said O'Ryan smiling. He gazed at her rapturously, as though she, an angel, would carry him off to heaven.

She smiled back at him with a bright look, twisted her hands together, raised her shoulders and sighed.

O'Ryan started to drift towards her. 'Your father said I might visit you,' he stuttered. Again he stood staring at her in wonder. She was so extraordinarily beautiful, he could not stop himself just looking, and any desire to speak went out of his head.

Again she glanced at him shyly, laid her head slightly on one side and gave a little bounce in the bed as if to a chuckle.

O'Ryan sadly considered that he ought to try and talk. 'I wanted to say how much I enjoyed your drawings,' he ventured looking down at them appreciatively. 'They are so colourful — though black and white. And Greek too! Especially the figures. But the landscape are too. You're so clever! How do you manage — in bed?' O'Ryan laughed and tailed off inanely. He gave up the idea of talking, and just stared at her again. The room was so still, he was at ease, at rest in himself, contemplating the goodly happiness of beauty.

The girl sighed again and shrugged now, with her head on one side like a beautiful clown. Then she beckoned to a chair by the bed. O'Ryan came and sat with her tenderly, seeming to float in her presence. Like a starved beggar at a deserted bakery he gazed. There was a wonderful oval quality to the shape of her forehead right down to her chin that made him think she had been sucked smooth like butterscotch. Her nose was fine, Grecian and straight, and her eyes perfect almonds, lidded with fragrant magnolia petals. Her silver brow was intellectual, and the eyebrows darted up like fishes, playing alternately with frowns or surprise. Her mouth bloomed. Although it opened and stretched now and then to a teasing smile, when at rest it brooded nurselike over a pointed chin. O'Ryan longed to leap madly forward and cover it all in a thousand kisses. His lips felt like butterflies demented at a feast of flowers.

'I saw both you and your father the other day,' he said eagerly. 'Taking a stroll in the Botanical Gardens. I don't know if you remembered me there, but you looked at me and smiled. I have thought of that smile for ever since. Your father is a wonderful man. He is my teacher, my guru. I can see I was destined by great good fortune to meet him. But when I saw you, it was like remembrance. Miss Alting, you are so beautiful! Your face was there at the beginning of Time. I saw your face, and I was like your knight, your pupil, your poet. I am yours, as in the old days of Gothic love.'

O'Ryan ended laughingly, staring with comedy in his face into hers also lit with laughter. Her humorous expression showed that she took his fervour in good heart. She screwed up her mouth, as if meditating some reprimand for such boldness, her eyebrows knitted together in mocking anger, but then she let fall her head in a kind of bright sob of laughter, and sighed as she enjoyed the foolery of his fancy.

Then she picked up some of O'Ryan's poems. She gave them to him, and pointed to him, then to her throat and mouth, and then with revolving finger at her ear.

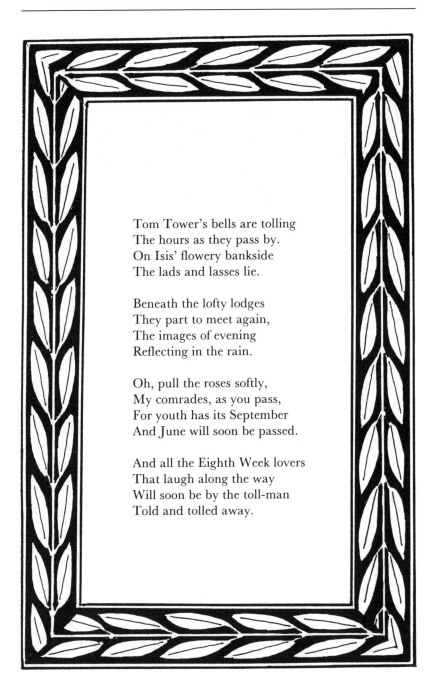

Tom Tower's bells are tolling
The hours as they pass by.
On Isis' flowery bankside
The lads and lasses lie.

Beneath the lofty lodges
They part to meet again,
The images of evening
Reflecting in the rain.

Oh, pull the roses softly,
My comrades, as you pass,
For youth has its September
And June will soon be passed.

And all the Eighth Week lovers
That laugh along the way
Will soon be by the toll-man
Told and tolled away.

Now over Oxford strangely the sun descends,
and through the twilight spreads the song
of thrushes,
mists breed among the lonely hillsides,
and from the darkness are fleeing huntsmen.

Now I remember the striped summer days of old,
days made of idleness with the easy creatures,
and once a journey south from Albion,
Lulu and I and the fount Alpheus,

even to jade-oceaned Sicily's domain,
and Etna's arms, where Isola Bella nighs,
in steepy town lying benighted,
while cockerels hammered out the grey dawn.

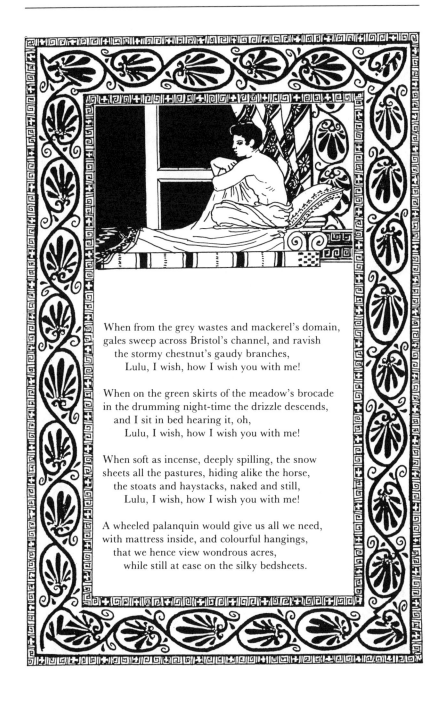

When from the grey wastes and mackerel's domain,
gales sweep across Bristol's channel, and ravish
   the stormy chestnut's gaudy branches,
      Lulu, I wish, how I wish you with me!

When on the green skirts of the meadow's brocade
in the drumming night-time the drizzle descends,
   and I sit in bed hearing it, oh,
      Lulu, I wish, how I wish you with me!

When soft as incense, deeply spilling, the snow
sheets all the pastures, hiding alike the horse,
   the stoats and haystacks, naked and still,
      Lulu, I wish, how I wish you with me!

A wheeled palanquin would give us all we need,
with mattress inside, and colourful hangings,
   that we hence view wondrous acres,
      while still at ease on the silky bedsheets.

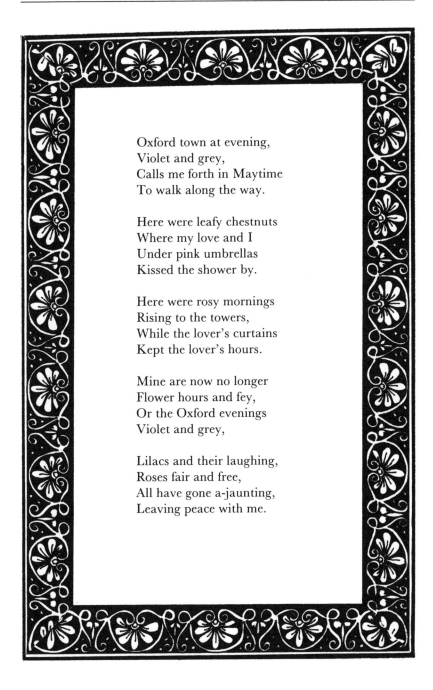

Oxford town at evening,
Violet and grey,
Calls me forth in Maytime
To walk along the way.

Here were leafy chestnuts
Where my love and I
Under pink umbrellas
Kissed the shower by.

Here were rosy mornings
Rising to the towers,
While the lover's curtains
Kept the lover's hours.

Mine are now no longer
Flower hours and fey,
Or the Oxford evenings
Violet and grey,

Lilacs and their laughing,
Roses fair and free,
All have gone a-jaunting,
Leaving peace with me.

Chapter Six

F og and noise enveloped the house of Number Eleven Foxview Road. The doors were all flung open, as were many of the windows, and men were clattering to and fro from its halls. Great desks and chairs and lamps and paintings were being lugged from floors and torn from walls; dust-covered, creaking objects were being trundled down staircases, through corridors and bundled out into the freezing air, while voices were calling, thumps were echoing: it was as if butchers were slugging and sawing into a carcase, whose entrails felt the cold fog billowing in, turning the cosy, old heart to stone.

Two large pantechnicons were rammed into the garden, as the crowds of removal men clumped about in them. Dark, stained blankets were flung over antiques, and straps were fitted round to hold them steady. Sideboard and wardrobe were wedged into place, and large cardboard boxes of wrapped china were set beside them. In jeans and thick jumpers and wearing protective gloves, the men flowed in a stream of exodus from an ancient world.

Hurrying to and fro among these lines there scurried Dr Fobey, his eyes lit with a forceful light of purpose. As if with revenge he eyed the precious antiques wrenched away, and the sad, personal hats and walking-sticks torn from their dusty old slumber. Dodging past him in the headlights and spotlights which had been turned on to combat the mist, the men moved in two sorts of moods: those swaying forth from the house betraying strained faces at either ends of dust-filmed tables or sofas, their heads revolving as they tried to avoid denting doors or knocking over

145

table-tops; those bouncing towards the house showing the light, disconnected look of the putters-down-of-heavy-loads. The face of Dr Fobey, neither strained, nor relaxed, was going and coming with a busy sense of relish.

'Ah, not those!' he called out, as a pair of men came bumping through the hall with a revolving bookcase of Edwardian design. 'That will count as books, and I want all books to remain exactly where they are, whether Metabas come or not!' Dr Fobey cast a look behind him as he said this, where the fog enveloped the garden, and the drive disappeared towards the gate. He strolled a few paces towards it, then ran along the drive through the mist, so that the lights and lorries and house faded away from him.

When he got to the end of the drive, peeping out from the decayed gate, which had already received a giant scar in its side from being scraped by a lorry, he looked out onto the fog-bound road, but having stared both east and west for some time, he saw no signs of any lights approaching in the fog. He lurched a look sharply down at his watch once more, cursed under his breath and threaded his way back to the blazingly-misted house.

The windows one either side of the front door had been opened to allow the dust to blow away, but since there was no breeze on this heavily becalmed morning, the dust cast up by the removal merely added to the veils. It was a sketch of a day, where the drawing which made up the universe was rubbed into blurs and continually being redraughted. Billowing up like snowstorms the dust created a cosmos of vapour and new creations emerged unsteadily from chaos. Oval or soft or rectangular, the newly-minted objects were tentatively paraded from the smoke.

But Dr Fobey was anxious now. He went into the house, and checked that the books were being left alone. Just as he suspected, he found that they were not, as he caught some removal men emptying a low bookcase onto the floor.

'I thought I gave clear instructions that the books were not to be touched,' said Fobey.

'We're not touching the books,' said the removal man adroitly.

'You most certainly are!' said Fobey with vim. 'You are putting them on the floor. But they are to stay in their shelves and cases, until Metabas arrive and deal with them. There's plenty of other furniture you can be attending to before you get down to the bookcases. Please try and stick to my instructions!'

The removal men sighed, as those do who have to deal with dons, and left the room, which was now empty of all but books.

'Kindly will no one touch any bookcases or empty any book-shelves,' called Fobey, as he followed the men about their tasks. 'And please do not disturb either the detachable labels on the bookcases and or those on the shelves, nor do not brush off the chalk-markings on the doors indicating the code-number of the room. These have all been arranged for the Metabas removal men, and you will note that A is the parlour, B is the study, C is any of the hallways, D the dining room, E the drawing room, F.G.H.I the chief bedrooms. So please try and remember that is the system.'

He went up to a shelf in the study, and with a prim sigh adjusted a little stuck-on piece of paper with the letter B 4.

There was the noise of an engine. Fobey flew into the hall and raced out of the front door. A large truck with headlights gleaming was lurching in through the gate. As it came towards them, the sign on its front declaimed Metabas Moves. Dr Fobey set his face in a frown, and marched towards it angrily, waiting with uplifted face for the driver to open the door of his cabin.

'You are two hours late!' he said to the driver, when he allowed access. 'I thought I said to start at seven-thirty.'

The driver did not speak. He switched off the engine, looked in the mirror and turned round to adjust something in the rear of his cab. Then he climbed out.

'Are you Dr Fobey?'

'Yes. Now please get a move on. We want this whole transport-ation completed today. What kept you?'

'What kept us?' the driver looked sourly at Fobey, as another car drew up behind the lorry. Five big men started clambering out of its tiny seats. 'Maybe you haven't noticed it's foggy?' said the driver.

'Certainly I have noticed the fog,' said Fobey, not backing down. 'But I got here none the less!'

'You didn't get here from Andover,' said the driver. With a sigh, he watched his mates getting themselves in order, then turned to Fobey with a sour look. 'If you must know,' he said, 'we had this fucking fog, then a blow-out on the motorway, and finally coming along just this road outside here, this weird woman leapt out in front of us, and tried to flag us down.'

Fobey felt a chill grip him. 'A woman. What sort of woman? What happened?'

The man bit up with his lower teeth onto the ends of his moustache. 'Well, we thought we'd hit her.'

Dr Fobey went white. The driver moved away, and shook his head commiseratingly with his comrades. 'Bloody lunatic,' he sighed. 'Did you find her?'

The others shook their heads.

'It's too foggy,' said one. 'But you couldn't've hit her anyways. She'd be flat out in the verge!'

The driver looked worried. Fobey came up beside him. 'What sort of a woman was it?'

They didn't answer.

'Perhaps I have misunderstood you,' continued Fobey urgently. 'A woman flagged you down. And I understand came near enough for you to worry that you might have hit her. Did you feel her hit the lorry or hear a thump?'

'No.'

'Then what sort of a woman was it?' Fobey was emphatic.

'Bloody weird, if you ask me,' said the driver. 'They saw her too, so I'm not making it up.' He paused and thought, then looked at the others for confirmation. 'She'd got a kind of false face, or something, and weird clothes, all patterns. And kind of stilts or big boots.'

Fobey looked startled. He stood for some time paralysed.

'OK, what about these books?' said the driver, the others ranged round on either side of him.

But Fobey was having difficulty calming himself. Once more he felt the terror that so far he had been happy to avoid, and a nagging sense of dismay tugged at his heart.

'Come on. What's the drill?' said the lorry-driver sharply.

Fobey woke out of his trance. 'Yes,' he said, 'follow me. We must get it done as quickly as possible. We must above all things be out of the house before nightfall!'

*   *   *   *

'Dr Alting,' said Dr Snare on the phone to the emeritus fellow, as the weird, misty light of the November morning shone on the work-notes on his desk, 'a Mr O'Ryan. I understand he is now in your charge, and that he reported to you for a tutorial this last Tuesday? While the President is away, I thought I ought to keep check on the matter. I was wondering how he shaped up in the tutorial, whether his essay was adequate, and what you thought of him academically?'

'Mr O'Ryan,' said the voice. There was a pause.

'An English Literature student, who was passed onto you in this late stage of the term. A gypsy-looking character, wears a bottle-green jacket. I was wondering what you thought of his progress?'

'Rather difficult to say,' said the voice.

'Well, he is a difficult student, I agree, and far from first class calibre. But what opinion did you form of him?'

'Of Mr O'Ryan?'

'O'Ryan, yes. A dark, curly-haired student. Look, how many students have you got?' Snare was resorting to sarcasm, but then had a thought. 'You did see him on Tuesday?'

There was a pause. Then a little cough. Then the precise, high-pitched voice said, 'Not exactly, no. I have been wondering what to do about it. I have taken certain action. But I rather thought he was due to meet me in the Oscar Wilde Room. Of course all this might not have occurred, if I had had my old room in the college, which was of course was far more suitable as a tutorial —'

'Just a moment,' Dr Snare spoke sharply. 'Am I to understand that O'Ryan did not show for his tutorial?'

'Possibly I misunderstood the place of assignation.'

'I really don't think so, Dr Alting. It was quite clear that it was to be in the Oscar Wilde Room.'

'Ah yes, I thought it was,' the voice sounded more confident. 'And at ten o' clock?'

Snare sighed, rolled his eyes up to the ceiling and said precisely, 'No, at eleven.'

'Ah, *hinc illae lacrimae!*' said the prim voice with some affectation of languor.

Dr Snare disliked both the languor and the Latin. He gritted his teeth. 'But were you there at eleven also?'

'I really can't remember.' said the languorous voice. Then thoughtfully it continued, 'I didn't have another pupil, and I wouldn't have had any cause to linger in that room in particular. I suppose I must have waited a statutory fifteen minutes or so, concluded he had not come and after glancing about the room a few times, left. I think I did drop a note to the President, though of course, being away, he would not yet have received it.'

'This is outrageous!'

'Well, really,' the voice startled into adopting a bleating tone, 'if I have only had my old room I am quite certain that —'

'Not you, Dr Alting,' snapped Snare. 'I'm talking about O'Ryan. I am afraid this is just completely unacceptable! I'll get onto the Senior Tutor. I don't think we need anyone else. In the President's absence, the authority for this sort of thing goes to the Senior Tutor, and he'll back me up for sure. O'Ryan has been repeatedly warned about this. The President himself told him that if it ever happened again, he would be dismissed. There is no doubt that it has happened on the first possible opportunity.'

'But I really don't think —'

'Look, Dr Alting, this is nothing for you to worry about. He didn't come to the tutorial, and you can be the witness of that. You've written to the President. Maybe you could send me a note over now on college notepaper, confirming that O'Ryan missed his tutorial? The only thing that would need to be done is that O'Ryan will have to be carefully questioned, and I shall do that myself. So please don't tell anyone of this business, and don't on any account speak to O'Ryan. He must *not* be forewarned. And he must *not* know about the mix up over the times. In fact I think it would be better if you kept this business of the time of the tutorial completely to yourself. So thank you, Dr Alting. I'd appreciate a brief note from you just confirming that O'Ryan missed his tutorial, and you needn't concern yourself any further!'

Snare slammed the phone down in an exultant rage, and with a determined look on his face seized on a sheet of notepaper and started writing.

* * * *

The transport truck of Metabas Moves was pulled up with its ramp down in the front quadrangle of St Mary's, and the book-laden men were now staggering out of its dim maw. The fog was thicker down in afternoon Oxford, and once more the lights blazed the mist, illuminating all about them the mysterious stones of the college. Gothic windows speared the gloom, decorated niches hung on walls, and a little outdoor pulpit floated hesitantly in the corner. The grand perpendicular style archway looked down myopically at the men who went like troglodytes into the stairway entrance that took them up to the SCR.

Fobey was dancing around like a bladderless fool in a Medieval procession, directing the stolid, bad-tempered porters here and there, though with little effect. Sometimes he would dash into an archway moments before they went with their loaded buckets, and having squeezed in first, clatter up the stairs again to watch with evil glee the ever-growing piles of books tipped out to swamp the library floor. Sometimes he would zigzag down the stairs after the bulky swaying men, and dart out again into the foggy quad only to stare about the college with something like guilty energy. At one point it was the lodge itself that he dashed into.

'Any sign of Dr Snare yet?' he said to the porter.

The porter looked up from his newspaper, slowly put it down, slowly went to the glass partition of the reception area, slowly opened it, and said, 'Good afternoon, Dr Fobey. Was there something?'

'I said: you're sure Dr Snare hasn't come back yet from the Faculty Meeting?'

'I haven't seen him, sir.' The porter shook his head, then looked bland.

'Well, I've something urgent to discuss with him. And you can see where I am. Tell him.'

'Yes, sir. Just one thing: the lorry. I didn't have an entry in the book about it, and I was just wondering if it was going to be there right up to evensong, because —'

'No, no!' said Fobey tetchily and zipped away again.

This time he poured himself into the doorway just ahead of a group of three men, and galloped up to the staircase, through the SCR and into the library, whose pointed-arched windows, looking out onto the fog, gave the place an air of startled holiness.

The librarian was pondering over the scene all rather aghast, stroking his pepper-and-salt beard and occasionally running a thin, pale hand over his bald head. Dr Fobey flung an index finger at one container and said, 'These are K. I think they all relate to the Peloponnesian War. So I suggest they go alongside the Ancient Historians.'

He started forth, then turned and said, 'Unless you think all the ancient historical texts ought to be kept in a separate position.'

'Oh, I'll just have to sort all that out later,' sighed the librarian.

Three more men, buckling at the knees with the weight of the book-buckets, trundled in and dropped their burdens with an 'Ooof' apiece. As Fobey and the librarian watched, two of them emptied out the books into shelf-like rows on the floor, their spines facing inwards. But the third held a bucket which was filled with cardboard boxes.

'Loose papers?' he said.

'They better go on the table,' said the librarian.

Fobey stared suspiciously, as the removal-man took them over, and then slid down a row of cardboard boxes onto the large, red-leather-covered table, whose top had been cleared of its usual display of periodicals. Amongst small files, off-prints and folders, there now lay a box which had loose sheets in, the top sheaf of which showed a drawing and a poem encased in a black and white Greek-patterned border.

* * * *

The mist had not lifted by the afternoon, as O'Ryan, having spent a delightful day in reading Petrarch, made his way to St Mary's from his lodgings. It was a perfectly still day, and the stillness and happiness in O'Ryan seemed to be matched by the suspended beauty of the weather. The fog had given to all around him a sense of intimacy and closeness, as though the vast world was really small, cosy and protected. It was as if a deep, tubular pool existed in which Oxford was at the bottom, while at the top was heaven in radiant blue. It seemed perfectly natural and undeniable that the earth was constructed in this fashion, and as soon as he moved out of the house, the celestially-crowned cylinder moved with him.

There was also something else which O'Ryan noticed. As the fog was accompanied by sharp cold, a furry frost had appeared on everything. A thick and glittering rime had bedecked all objects in the gardens, as the mist first condensed then froze in microscopic feathers. Like a great choreographer the frost drilled the mass of life into form, and made Oxford a great stage filled with a *corps de ballet* in sparkling white uniform. Meanwhile in the orchestra pit each gate, each wall, each piece of pavement, each lingering rose was smokily orchestrated in icy harmonies.

Through a hushed, pure world thus O'Ryan moved and turned his frost-ghostly bike by the looming shadow of the silent church. And in secrecy and silence he went under chestnut-trees whose darkness overhead was criss-crossed by hoary twigs and powdered leaves. Through a city converted to reverence he pedalled gently and meanderingly and sighed to see pinnacles and turrets by fog-rime refined. A heart-snatching fairness had aged the city, and made it a place of spirits.

The chief reason, of course, for O'Ryan feeling so at one with this most delicate of days was that he had been transformed by his encounter on the hill. After his meeting with love and learning, O'Ryan felt new born. A delightful sense of goodness, washedness and childishness gripped him. He looked at the city as if there had been revealed to him a secret festival in which the world partook on days never before noticed. He looked around on cafés and shops, as if seeing them suddenly pranked and garlanded, their shoppers all with presents under their arms, striding their way to trysts in lamplit attics, or home with port and chocolates for a special day. Yes, it was the late Michaelmas Term festival, the famous late November Wednesday, when all the world was tender-hearted and glad!

When the wall of St Mary's appeared beneath the mist-staining traffic-lights, O'Ryan got off his bike and went to park it in his usual place. But then he found that the main gate was open, and a great lorry had driven in and was unloading cases into the college. He stared for a while at the strange procession of bucket-bearing removal men, but then left his bike and went into the lodge. The lights burnt cheerily by the glass and ledgers and mail-boxes and notices, and the porter sat calmly reading his newspaper. A sunny and reverent greeting gave O'Ryan, then he looked into his pigeon-hole, and saw he had received a letter bearing the college crest.

When he opened this letter, and read it in a corner of the lodge, he found that Dr Snare wished to see him at once. O'Ryan was surprised, and then strangely cheered, for in his present mood he sensed a reconciliation. Probably Dr Alting had spoken of how well they had got on, and how receptive he had found his new student, and how it was wonderful to find a student who was interested in old-fashioned things like learning and discipline and form and poetry. And Dr Snare having learnt of these matters had felt a change of heart and realised that he had misjudged Nigel O'Ryan.

'Ah, the born poet!' said a voice, as if in confirmation of these meditations.

O'Ryan looked up and saw Ramsey and Fosdyke and Bergson clustering round him.

'Trouble, is it?' said Bergson sombrely, pointing at the letter O'Ryan was considering.

'No,' said O'Ryan, 'far from it actually. Dr Snare has asked to see me.'

'Sounds bad to me.'

'Why should it be?'

'Search me. How went your tute?'

O'Ryan smiled. 'It was wonderful! It was so lovely and heartening. It was a place of safety, after a long night on a stormy sea!'

There was a pause while they stared at him.

'Wonderful, eh?'

The others sniggered.

'Lovely and heartening?'

'A safe port after a stormy sea?'

They snorted. 'OK. Now pull the other one!'

But O'Ryan didn't react.

Fosdyke at length sneered 'You didn't catch cold then, sitting out in the rain?'

O'Ryan frowned. 'What are you talking about?'

'Your tute with Alting! You might as well admit it. Damn it, we all know what happened!'

O'Ryan stared from one to the other. 'You know what happened! But how can you?' He paused. 'I haven't spoken about it to anyone yet. And Dr Alting wouldn't tell anyone.' He bit his lip, then had a sudden happy thought. 'Wait a minute! Have you been talking to Sumpter? Do you know Sumpter? Is he at a college here? Did you know *I* knew him?'

'What the hell are you talking about?'

'This is getting bizarre!'

'Who the fuck is Sumpter?'

O'Ryan's face fell. 'Oh, it wasn't him then?'

'Who wasn't him? Look, what is all this drivel?'

'Well, whoever told you I had a wonderful tutorial! I mean, I couldn't have hoped for a better tutor. Dr Alting was the very man I had been dying to meet. I got a lifetime of teaching in just one hour. It was so strange. It was like a dream really. He just told me everything I needed to know. He really is a most wonderful man!'

There was a pause, then the others started shuffling and grinning. 'Oh, all right!' they said, 'Very good, very funny. Well done, O'Ryan. You've put up a good act, and *almost* had us fooled.'

'Yes, a clever ploy, O'Ryan, and following the maxim that attack is the best form of defence!'

'He's not one to be dashed. You've got to hand it to him. If he hadn't laid it on so thick, I might have believed him.'

They all nodded and smiled coldly at O'Ryan, who was still trying to understand what was behind their words.

But then Fosdyke said menacingly, 'Convincing Snare, though, won't be so easy!' He levelled a look at O'Ryan, pursed his lips and shook his head.

The gang started to drift off towards the JCR, leaving the lodge and disappearing into the lorry-lit mist.

O'Ryan stared after them, then dodged the streams of removal men to catch up with them on the entrance to the cloisters. He was perplexed. 'Look, wait a minute!' he called, and the group turned and waited for him to catch up.

But Dr Fobey came out of the entrance and peered into the lorry at the shrinking collection of book-buckets.

'What is all this about?' said O'Ryan to the others. 'You knew I had to see Dr Alting, and I went up to his house in Boar's Hill. And I had a wonderful time. And I even met his daughter too.'

'Oh go to hell, O'Ryan! Look, we know you've been had, so why keep on trying to cover it up?'

'What the fuck are you talking about?'

'You never saw Dr Alting!'

'I did!'

'You didn't! He was waiting for you down here. We saw him wandering around after the time fixed for your tute wondering where on earth his student was. I mean he gets things muddled anyway. But you stood him up, and that's why Snare is gunning for you.'

O'Ryan stared at them, and they stared at him.

'Oh Christ, here he is!'

Dr Snare himself approached, coming from the Holywell Quad, his head deep in reading a file. The others made a quick drift off into the shadowy archways. O'Ryan stood still baffled.

Fobey, with his hand on the edge of the removal van, called out to the approaching tutor. 'Dr Snare!'

Snare stopped and looked up.

'I would like to have an urgent talk with you,' said Fobey. 'I left a message to this effect in the lodge, but they swore you had not yet returned. It's about the Estates Committee tomorrow. Are you free to talk?'

But Snare looked past him. 'Mr O'Ryan,' he called. 'I left an urgent note for you in the lodge. Did you get it?'

'Er — yes,' said O'Ryan, coming up quietly.

'And did you intend to come and see me?'

'I was just on my way,' said O'Ryan.

'Through the cloisters?' sneered Snare.

Snare glowered a while, then turned to Fobey with his mouth open, and made an intake of breath.

But Fobey spoke first. 'Perhaps you could attend to Mr O'Ryan first, then come up to see me in the SCR library?' he said. 'I would rather we didn't have to rush. And I think you'll be amused by what I have to show you. I'll be there for at least another hour.'

Dr Snare nodded to Dr Fobey, then looked at the undergraduate. 'Shall we go to my room?' He led the way.

* * * *

'Now,' said Dr Snare, when he had settled in behind his desk, and left O'Ryan to stand on the carpet in front of it. 'I think we need to have a very serious talk.' He opened a drawer in his desk, bent down to it, did something which made a clicking noise and brought out a file which he placed on the top. Then he licked his lips, made little wriggling gestures with his fingers, and said, 'Now, Mr O'Ryan, with regard to your present standing in the college. There are a number of things that I need to know. But just let me ask you this to begin with. How did you get on in your tutorial with Dr Alting?'

'Oh, very well.'

'Really?'

'Yes, extremely well in fact. I was just telling my friends about it.'

Snare worked his mouth, as if getting it ready for a statement of supreme precision. But then he couldn't help himself giving a little grin of plebeian satisfaction. 'No problems of any kind?' he said at last sprucely.

'Oh, none at all. I got on with him like a house on fire.'

Dr Snare sat back in his chair, pulled his coat and tie and stared at O'Ryan. 'Right,' he said firmly. 'Then let's just go over this a bit. You went to see him promptly on Tuesday morning?'

'Oh yes, I wouldn't be late.'

'And what time did you go?'

'The time you told me: eleven o' clock.'

Snare worked his mouth to cover a small, triumphant smirk. 'I see.' As if making a prize-winning snooker-stroke, Snare stared level ahead and said, 'And he was there at eleven prompt himself?'

'Of course,' O'Ryan thought a while.

Snare frowned to see it.

'Well, maybe he came along fractionally a bit after,' said O'Ryan.

'How long after?'

'Not more than five minutes.'

'So a perfectly normal tutorial meeting, with student and tutor showing up at eleven o' clock?'

'Yes.' O'Ryan was beginning to sense something was wrong.

Snare sneered with malicious triumph and then said, 'I'm sorry, O'Ryan, but I'm afraid I know it's not quite like that. In fact the truth is very far from what you have claimed. What would you say, for instance, if I suggested that Dr Alting never saw you on Tuesday at all?'

'I'd say you were mistaken. He was there all right. We had a wonderful tute and I read him my essay and he liked it. I think he enjoyed the way I had dealt with the drama, and how Shakespeare managed to build up the scenes to a pitch of dramatic tension, by cunningly delaying —'

'Look, Mr O'Ryan, I've had a whole year or so of your theories and your approach to literature, and I hate to tell you this, but it doesn't interest me in the slightest. In fact I find it profoundly boring. So let's restrict the literary discussion to a minimum. You say you had a tutorial with Dr Alting at eleven o' clock. I say I don't believe you. And believe me I can prove it too. Had you met Dr Alting before your tutorial with him?'

'No.'

'Ah. You'd never met him before at all?'

'No.'

Dr Snare was sneering excitedly, continually licking his lips as he shaped his cross-examination. 'Had you ever seen a photograph or a portrait of him?'

'No.'

'Ah!' said Snare jubilantly. 'Then what did he look like?' When no answer came, Snare grinned and waved a finger at O'Ryan in vulgar scorn. 'I reckon I've got you there, Mr O'Ryan!'

'Well, I had seen him before as a matter of fact,' said O'Ryan.

Snare's face fell and he looked angry.

'I hadn't met him before,' O'Ryan explained, 'but I had seen him.'

'Are you trying to fool with m —'

'Look, you said had I met him before? No! Had I seen a photo of him before? No! But had I seen him before? Yes!' O'Ryan sighed at the memory. 'I saw him once in the Botanical Gardens.'

Snare was looking slightly concerned.

'He was with his daughter, as a matter of fact. He was taking her in her wheel-chair around the gardens before the winter set in.'

'Oh,' said Snare, looking up sharply. 'I didn't know he had a daughter. So you had seen him before, so if you know what he looks like, maybe you could describe him to me? No wait a minute!' Snare thought of something else. 'Had you spoken to Dr Alting before you had your so-called tutorial with him?'

'No.'

'So until you had your so-called tutorial with him on Tuesday, you had not heard his voice?'

'No.'

'Right then!' said Snare incisively. 'What does his voice sound like?'

O'Ryan smiled as he considered Dr Alting's voice. 'Kindly,' he said, 'very deep, jovial-sounding.'

Snare sneered. 'You're lying to me, O'Ryan. You never saw Dr Alting. You never had a tutorial with him. You are making this up. His voice is not at all as you describe. It is a rather hurried, squeaky voice. I have just been speaking to him this morning on the phone. You are lying.'

O'Ryan stared at him puzzled and somewhat repulsed. 'Are you trying to set me up?' he said.

'What do you mean by that?'

'Well, you've been leading me on with all these questions, as though you fancy yourself as a barrister! What are you playing at? You're trying to set me up. You want to get rid of me. You've had one go, and this is your second attempt! And you're trying to prove I missed my tutorial with Dr Alting, which is a pretty dumb thing to do, because he's never going to back you up. Didn't you even ask him this morning how he got on in his tutorial with me?'

'Of course I did. Now listen to me, O'Ryan,' said Snare menacingly. 'You are in big trouble! And you're not getting out of it by fancy footwork. You've been warned by the President that if you are caught out once more with any misdemeanour you are going to be sent down, and I have to tell you, O'Ryan, that you have and will be! You know damn well you missed that tute, and you know damn well that you were warned by the President himself. You may have a crafty little plan for trying to shift the blame, but you don't floor me that easily. If you want to fight dirty, boy, I can fight dirty too, believe me!'

'Oh, it's your constant study!' said O'Ryan. 'If you spent more time trying to appreciate literature and less trying to rat your way up the academic hierarchy, you might be a better tutor!'

'You've got a bloody nerve! I'm recording this, you know!'

'Oh great! You'll scrub that bit off, no doubt! Well, you've got a bloody nerve too calling me a liar, and I don't care who you play that to! If you'd said I was a liar at Dr Arbuthnot's Grammar Academy, you'd've be called out to a duel with Masai spears, and quite honestly I wouldn't fancy your chances!'

'Look, I'm sorry, I've had enough of this! You're going to be sent down, and that's that! And threatening me with physical violence just clinches it as far as I'm concerned! And you can't deny it either because it's all here on tape. I'm glad other people will be able to hear your out-and-out Fascist attitude! This jibe about the Masai gives your game away, O'Ryan! You may think you're a wonderful Classicist and a sober disciplinarian, but I know better. There are thousands of people just like you in South Africa, and we don't want 'em here! Now get out!'

'Get out?' yelled O'Ryan. 'What are you raving about, you little prissy-lipped squirt? I was told to go to Dr Alting for a tutorial. I did. I read him my essay. He liked my essay. He gave me one for next week too and I'm going to read it to him! Why the fuck are you having nightmares about me being a Fascist? For Christ's sake, will you just come down off the ceiling, and talk sense?'

There was a long, cold silence. Snare looked down at his tape-recorder, controlled himself and said, 'I notice that you have made no reference to a mix up over the time of your tutorial. Dr Alting told me on the phone this morning that he expected you at ten and you didn't come. You might well have saved your skin by saying that you went at eleven for your tutorial, found no one there, and came away again. But you didn't. You were foolish enough to claim that you went to the tutorial at eleven and actually met Dr Alting there, a Dr Alting whose voice is deep and musical, whereas in fact it is high-pitched and squeaky. Dr Alting is writing me a letter confirming that you did not go to the tutorial. You missed it, didn't report the matter, and then when confronted actually lied and claimed that you went: this is the reason, Mr O'Ryan, why you are going to be sent down.'

Snare paused for a while, and studied O'Ryan's white face closely. He adjusted his lips a few times, saw with pleasure that no answer was forthcoming, and so with a sham sigh of weariness continued. 'Now I have spoken to the Senior Tutor, and he is in agreement with me that while the President is away, we have to take action ourselves on behalf of the college. I can therefore tell you officially that you are dismissed from this college and this will mean that you are simultaneously and with immediate effect dismissed from Oxford University. Your local authority will be informed by means of an official letter which should be in their hands by the end of next week, and you will have to come to some arrangement with them over repaying them your grant. This will amount to a figure of undoubtedly some five figures, and although I believe you have qualified for a grant, I suspect your father will have some funds suitably stowed away in South Africa, and the sum won't ruin the family, but even so, I'm sure he's not going to pleased. So maybe from now on, O'Ryan, you'll try to listen when people give you advice. It only remains for you to have a brief meeting with the President on his return next Monday at four o' clock.' Snare sneered. 'You will then leave Oxford at once.'

O'Ryan stared at Dr Snare. Then he said, 'Will you just phone up Dr Alting, please, and check with him? I know he will not deny that he had a tutorial with me.'

'Is that so?' said Snare.

'Yes,' said O'Ryan.

'Then we'll see, shall we?'

With an angry look Snare dialled Dr Alting's number.

After a pause, some one answered the other end. 'Oh, Mrs Alting?' said Snare. 'I was wondering if your husband were at home? There's just something further I'd like to discuss with him concerning our conversation this morning.'

The phone replied.

Dr Snare said, 'Thank you.'

Snare did not look at O'Ryan, as they both waited for Dr Alting to be fetched, with the fog outside the window getting thicker, and the day starting to fade.

Dr Snare was nervous but confident. O'Ryan, however, already felt his stomach sinking at having heard Snare talk to Mrs Alting. There was no Mrs Alting, as far as he knew.

'Ah, Dr Alting?' said Snare vivaciously. 'You remember we were discussing just this morning how a Mr O'Ryan failed to turn up for his tutorial on Tuesday? . . . That's it. . . . Now I just want to check with you that you are quite sure you did not see him. . . . You're quite sure of that? . . . Good. Yes, well, I have him here, and I think it might be best if you could just say that to him yourself.'

Snare looked away and handed the phone to O'Ryan.

O'Ryan seized the phone and said with some desperation and all in a rush, 'Dr Alting? I'm sorry about all this bother. I can't think what has caused it. But you must remember the tutorial we had yesterday, and my essay on *Othello*, and my poems we talked about, and how you asked me to stay for a while and talk to your d —'

O'Ryan broke off. Some one was cutting in on him, and he found himself listening to a totally foreign voice expressing astonishment, and being told that Dr Alting had neither a daughter nor any recollection of seeing poems, essay or person of O'Ryan.

O'Ryan handed back the phone and stared into space.

'So, time to go,' sneered Snare.

Chapter Seven

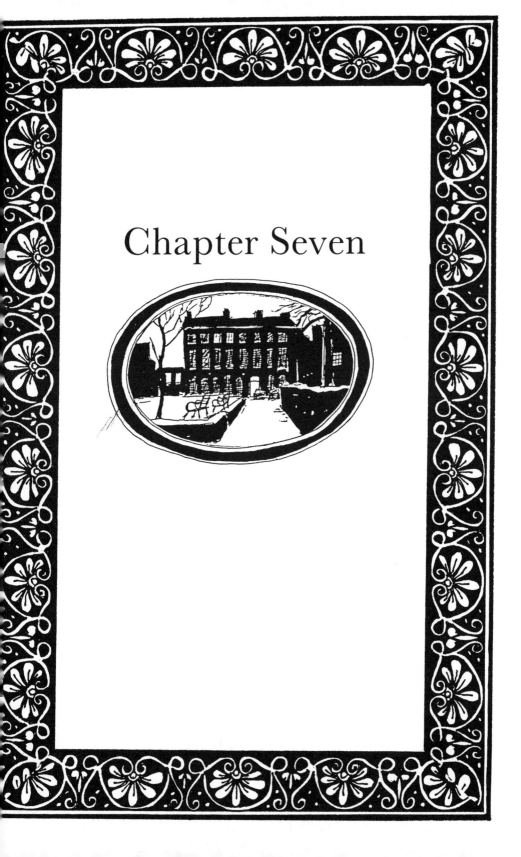

In the frosty fog the monkey-puzzle tree shot from the ground with bizarre optimism, then engulfed by the dusk lost its mysterious head. Its weird spikey arms, leaved like lizard-scales, like garlands swagged, hung bravely among the grey vapours of twilight, but its sturdy, central trunk merely faded and faded in the air, until the pole of its bole vanished. O'Ryan stood beneath, perplexed like the tree, unable to see its top or the ground, as the dying day and the mist took away everything. He was stunned by the loss of his Oxford life, puzzled like the monkeys of the tree's name, who might gaze up at the spikey trunk of progress, but know that they were barred from climbing. The pain of banishment mingled with the nobility of the tree to produce a bitter time among the beautiful.

As he walked through the cypresses and shrubs along the gravel paths and by the iced-over ponds of the Botanical Gardens, O'Ryan felt bereft in Eden. It was as though he was locked in paradise and although shut off from the fallen world, which busily and aggressively got on without him, was yet saddened and maddened by exclusion from the wild outside. Sadly also the clumps of Michaelmas daisies before which had passed his fancied love and tutor, and sadly the sumptuous pastel-flamed gladioli whose hues were then unfurling, reminded him that even the dream had decayed, for the flowers were all blackened and withered in the day's end, blasted in the white earth, preserved by rime in the state of putrefaction, while the rest of the garden pursued its noble burgeoning, its tall trees framed by neo-classical stone.

It was a topsy-turvy world that O'Ryan bereftly trod, encountering each shrub or rhododendron bush solitarily. It was a world of blanket mist, which alone seemed to have reality, and in whose dusk all tangible objects were lost like ghosts. And in this land of fog the very weight of matter began to seem unreal, stranded on the shore, as though waiting for the sea or removal men to come and snatch it, and O'Ryan clutched his folder to his breast, trying to keep something lost in ghostland, while Snare and the college and the lorry and his friends were all sniggering outside in brash reality, and he locked in the place where immediate things were distant and everlasting mysteries here and now.

O'Ryan found he had strolled through the archway, beneath the frost-embroidered clematis, to where the great greenhouses rose up with their arches of glass. Along by the wall the rime-covered cobwebs waved like lace over the pleached peach trees, while on the other side the windows were steamy of the tropical world. On the frost-sheeted path, by the rimy pods of the leaf-falling laburnum O'Ryan walked a little longer in frost-land. Then through the shaking door he passed into a damp-smelling, flower-pot-littered world, where slimy green moss and sweating leaves hung about him.

The lush, warm palms that burgeoned and flourished in the Equatorial world, and the pale-pink lotuses, steeping the tips of their petals in magenta, these brought him now a feeling of earthiness, of growth and sappy life, and he sighed to stroke his hands through the reeds in the dark, auburn, stem-threaded water. The clear warm water lapped at the edges of the pool, themselves furry with moss, and tiny-stemmed flowers sprouted from jewelled patches. A motherly warmth of Mid-African splendour flowed all round O'Ryan, and at once he felt himself reassured and comforted.

O'Ryan looked down. In a clearing of his mind he stared for a while at the folder. Clutched to him in the garden, but now held relaxed, through its clear plastic cover it showed the page beneath. It was the bordered page he had found in the garden before, sporting a dolphin, and lit by delight his lips curled up in the corners. And at once O'Ryan looked to the centre of the pond where another dolphin sported, a bronze fountain, raising its beak

up over the lotuses. The jet of water splashed towards the south, just as his own dolphin pointed, and in the pond the goldfish and tench also streamed that way. He smiled to see the fishes and flowers tumbling towards southern hills, and felt that they bore his heart and yearning with them.

Then O'Ryan suddenly woke from this fancy. What was he doing just strolling here? Why had he let Snare strike him all of a heap? How had he allowed himself to be summarily banished from Oxford, to be sent down for attending a tutorial which for some reason or other no one knew of? He knew himself the tutorial had existed. He knew that he had received a letter re-arranging the venue. He knew that he could prove to Snare or the President that he was innocent of any oversight. All he needed to do was to get confirmation from his own particular Dr Alting that O'Ryan had read him his essay on *Othello*. Proof that he had attended a tutorial would show that he had not transgressed, and Snare would then be forced to revise his judgement.

Gathering his folder under his arm, and marching back to the door, he prised it open onto the cold, quiet air, then ran out of the greenhouse, along the path, through the misty gate, and across the bridge towards his frosted bicycle. Once on the road the lights of windows and car-headlights ambered the air, and bustle and colour came again to the evening. With the frost biting his ears, O'Ryan flung his folder in the basket, bestraddled the saddle, set off past the traffic-lights, and at once began heaving himself on high pedals up the long, curving High, whence the dolphin on his folder sported the way towards Foxview Road.

* * * *

'You don't think they'll over-rule your co-opting me on the committee?' said Snare.

'Certainly not,' said Fobey.

Snare and Fobey were standing together in the SCR library staring at the huge army of books. The lights were on from both ceiling and table, and were reflected in the windows, where the cold mist pressed having dissolved all sight of the college. The paper labels perched on the piles were looking battered from their trip, and some columns of books had slewed over into little avalanches. The eyes of Snare and Fobey revolved continually

about the literary landscape, but the two dons were not talking of
learning.

'There is no constitutional right for any objections,' continued
Fobey, his eyes piercing the idea, as he adjusted his glasses
proprietorially. 'As Chairman I have the power of co-opting
members for specific occasions. And the occasion for your presence will be declared. You will have been brought onto the
committee in the capacity of a literary expert, in order to make a
judgement of the worth of the Maeonides library. It will then be
incidental, and purely incidental that you have the power to vote
for the Hammerstein buildings.'

Snare thought for a while. Then he said, 'But Werble is a
literature don. Might he and they not feel you are casting doubt
on his authority?'

Fobey was contemptuous. 'Werble was brought onto the committee to be a dogsbody, and what's more to be an innocent
dogsbody. As he was new, like the President, and had no previous
knowledge of the Maeonides house, he was expected to negotiate
its sale without any prejudice. Unfortunately we seem to have
chosen someone particularly inept and vacillating. I think the
committee would appreciate a man of your forthright qualities.'

Snare thought again. 'And this vote on the quad is to be taken
at the next meeting?'

'It must be. We need to press ahead with the fund-raising
campaign. Unless we take a decision tomorrow a whole year's
appeal will be lost. It will also suggest that we are dithering. As I
see it, a majority of the committee are already in favour of the
Hammerstein quad, but I conceive it to be my duty to make sure
the right decision is taken. It is after all a matter of crucial
importance in the modern world not to back down to reactionary
resentment.'

Fobey broke off and stared for a while at the bookshelves which
held the work of the college fellows. 'By the way,' he continued,
'speaking of reactionary resentment: have you recently taken out
some library copies of Maeonides?'

'No way,' said Snare with a proletarian sneer.

The pair of dons relapsed into silence. There seemed to be a fair
amount of reactionary resentment among the covers of the
volumes before them. The dust and quiet of the old house had

cosseted so many tomes for so long that they had a raw look at being displaced and scraped by rough mechanicals, and they also retained some doubt as to whether they should allow themselves to be shut up in an elite library reserved for the contempt of the modish.

'Well, maybe I better have a look around,' said Snare. 'Though I must say the collection seems highly antique. A large helping of empire-building books seem to be the order of the day. Whenever I see one of those ghastly embossed, pictorial Edwardian covers, my stomach heaves at the picture it conjures of Kipling and colonial paternalism. I mean look at this: *A Primer of Hinduism* by J.N. Farquhar! Doesn't that say it all? It should have been called *Know Your Native, and Rule Him Better!*'

Sighing elaborately he then moved through the Classical Translations section, though not without also smearing them with disapproval. 'And all these Gilbert Murrays!' Snare sneered. 'Eliot, I think, saw him off to everyone's satisfaction, though reactionaries like Lewis tried to defend his ghastly translations. You know, I've had a quick look through the modern novels, and there's no Lawrence, no Woolf, no Joyce even! This man was really barely educated! And look at this section: Polti *Thirty-Six Dramatic Situations*, Freytag *On the Technique of the Drama*. I seem to remember a student of mine telling me that even the Bodleian doesn't have these, at least in their English versions. Honestly, the time people used to waste on these damn-fool topics! Thank God I managed to transfer that particular earnest postgraduate!'

Things grew quiet, as Snare relapsed into a study of more sections of the Maeonides library. He skirted round the piles in a rather uncertain and skittish manner, for he would peer closely at some, but then shy away from others. Not being a Classicist he was out of his depth with most of the assortment, though aware of them from companions and encyclopedias, and although he could rely on contempt to maintain his own confidence in conversation, it was not so easy when he was on his own. Fobey meanwhile stared into space thoughtfully. He was also having a number of doubts. He found that he had fallen into a rather vacant mood, after all the excitements of the day.

Snare had turned to the tables. These were now covered in cardboard boxes which bore loose papers and offprints. His eye had been caught by one containing a picture and some verse, decorated in a border with a black and white pattern. He looked at a landscape, surveyed a verse which began 'Who was it put in women's arms' and sniggered at its simplistic rhyming. The next page said 'Thor the thunderer', and was a sort of male-chauvinist's hymn, every bit as bad as A.E. Housman. Snare bit his lips with derisory laughter at what he took to be Maeonides quite dreadful attempts at writing modern verse, and then came on a page which was somewhat different in layout and style from the others. It was a page which he found disturbing. It had a large pair of double-doors drawn in black over most of the page. The doors were of a neo-classical design, as if to an Eighteenth Century ballroom, and underneath a very brief poem in the same simplistic style as the other verses. But as Snare looked, ready to sneer at the sing-song quality of the verse, something strange seemed to happen.

At first he thought the black on the page reflected something behind him, for he turned to look over his shoulder, as if expecting to see a face there whose image the ink had thrown up. But there was nobody. So he looked again at the drawing of the door. It did indeed seem to be a door, a door into another world. The black seemed to blend itself over the door, suggesting shapes, blurring with the darkness, so that the longer he stared at this darkness, the more it seemed to be filled with the strange reflected presences which had first caught his imagination.

He broke off and looked down again at the poem. Why this ponderous presentation? There was nothing remarkable about the verse. It was about roses. It seemed to be attempting to make a statement on the perennial appeal of the commonplace, but was really a piece of rather meaningless Romantic drooling about poetry's chief cliché. It made no statement. It had no thought. It was completely lacking in shock. It had no stance to posit to a modern reader. Yet why should it be linked to a door? Was this Eliot's door to the rose-garden? Maybe Maeonides had been stirred by Eliot's image and had tried to copy it? On the other hand maybe Maeonides was dead before Eliot wrote *The Four Quartets*. It was a highly boring little poem and in that ghastly antique, lyrical style which Snare hated. It seemed to be merely trying to be pretty, like the pastoral simperings of Herrick — as

Though you are gone, the rose remains,
The rose-bush and the red-thorn tree,
And in the memory this sustains
The soul of the rose remains with me.

though Donne hadn't exploded all that world for good! Snare turned away in disgust.

But then something drew him to the door again. It had dissolved, and with a start of horror he found he could see right through it. He was staring into a dark room. It was an old study, with a fire-place, a great high-backed chair by the fire, and two clocks on the mantlepiece on either side of the bust of an ancient old man. And all round the room were rows and rows of books, whose titles he could not see, and on the top shelf of the bookcases were nine statuettes of female figures. Snare was staggered at this. How could he possibly see into a book and see a room, complete with chairs and bookshelves? It was a hallucination. But he could see it clearly, though the room was dark, yet even that darkness was a strangely-glowing darkness, as of light. Far off outside through the fog a great blast of a truck's horn echoed from the bridge and over the college cloisters.

Suddenly Snare became even more engrossed. The room was not empty either. There were people in it! They were Victorian people! There was a woman with two pistols in her hand! And standing nearest to the chair was another woman, all decked out in lace and a crinoline with a crown on her head and a trumpet in her hand! And there was a young, beautiful girl, decked in faded velvets, with a flowered straw hat, a muff on one hand and in the other a sheet of piano-music. The three Nineteenth Century girls stood in strange and pompous poses, as though stiffly awaiting the men to retire from the dinner-table and notice them. And as Snare stared, they all turned to him and gazed myopically towards his face, as though watching him approach from a distance. Snare started back with terror at this vision.

As he did so, the sharp movement caused Fobey to look at him, and the Estates Bursar stared at him wonderingly. Fobey saw Snare backing away from a sheaf of papers with something like terror in his eyes. He looked at him, tried to attract his attention, but Snare was lost in another world. Fobey felt dread. He moved over to the sheaf of papers himself, and saw the black-and-white drawing of the door and the poem. He looked back at Snare. Snare was retreating into a corner of the room, staring now at Fobey with horror.

Fobey looked at the door again. What was so terrifying about

Though you are gone, the rose remains,
The rose-bush and the red-thorn tree,
And in the memory this sustains
The soul of the rose remains with me.

this picture, and the scrappy poem about roses underneath? He took another look at Snare, who was still speechless but indicating with his eyes for him to look and see what he could see. Fobey stared at the door. Strange, he thought: the ink seemed to be reflective. He could not help himself turning and looking over his shoulder. Was there something behind him, or was that a river somehow depicted on the ink? He could swear he could see a river. And also figures! But were the figures in the ink or behind him? He tensed his neck in dread at the thought. Were they looking over his shoulder? Were they breathing their cold breath down his neck? All at once he became terrified. He dare not turn round. Yet he knew there was nothing. It was the ink that threw up these images. Women on a bleak shore! But it was unreal! It must be a trick. He was fearful, but he was going to do it. He took another look at Snare.

Snare was watching him intently now, seeing that Fobey too was caught by the visions. But Snare saw Fobey do something that he himself had not dared to do. He saw him try to reach forward to the door and attempt to push it open. Snare felt like telling him not to do it. But then thought: why should he worry? He was over in the corner. He watched Fobey with a nasty stare of curious malevolence. It would be interesting to see what was going to happen. His curiosity was rewarded. From where he was huddled, it seemed that Fobey reached right into the book. The hand went right into the page! As the bursar's mouth grimaced open in horror, he was watching his own fingers going in, sinking deep into the black pit of ink. Then he tried to snatch them out again, but something seemed to freeze his whole body, and he could not withdraw his hand, even from a piece of paper.

Snare was fascinated and fearful. Fobey seemed to be wracked with horror and pain, and all from a page of paper and ink. The Estates Bursar was desperate in his struggle, yet he seemed to be struggling merely against a paralysis of himself. Snare none the less felt terrified now. He decided he had better go. He could tell the porter that Fobey was having trouble in the SCR library. He started to sidle away along the shelves, and exit without being seen. But as he did he knocked over a pile of books.

With a slithering noise like an animal lunging, the books toppled and crashed untidily all over the floorboards. With a

175

Though you are gone, the rose remains,
The rose-bush and the red-thorn tree,
And in the memory this sustains
The soul of the rose remains with me.

shout Fobey then drew back. He had retrieved his hand. The sound of books had broken the spell. Fobey ran at once to the door to the SCR. Snare ran after him. They threw open the door together, dashed into the common room, and slammed the door loudly behind them. Fobey tried to fit his key in the lock. His hands were shaking. He could not see it. He struggled panic-stricken. He did it.

When the door was locked, Fobey collapsed against the wall and looked at Snare with a huge sense of dismay. 'I should have left them there!' he cried. 'I meant to destroy them! But instead I've brought them down into Oxford! Oh, can't you see now? The prophecy is fulfilling: "When black is made white, the spirits will take revenge!"'

* * * *

It was evening as O'Ryan pedalled up the last long stretch of the road towards Boar's Hill. Though the mist thinned a little beyond the meandering waters of Isis, yet the winter dusk was plunging into darkness whatever on the slopes remained to be seen. Although the road had been salted, and the wet, russet-coloured patches darkened the tarmac, yet in the hedgerows the autumn grasses were frosted into quills, and beyond them in the mist the ragged hawthorns, with leaves fallen, were also berried with rime. Yet O'Ryan was not frozen. He pedalled with zest and energy. He was buoyed up by the comforting knowledge that *his* Dr Alting would surely set things right.

He had felt this from the first about his tutor. *His* Dr Alting was a man about whom grew a field of common sense. When hysteria flourished, and drastic action was about to be taken, his presence, he knew, would test things in the light of plainness. His merely being in a room would settle matters into a natural form, and shape would be revealed as if by a steady light. A word or two thus from *his* Dr Alting would clear up the matter of the missed tutorial, and release him from the harsh injunction. And O'Ryan also relaxed to think that thereafter he might revisit Miss Alting. And what a deal of drama he could tell her! How things had been shaken up! What ordeals her knight had passed through so soon after he had left her!

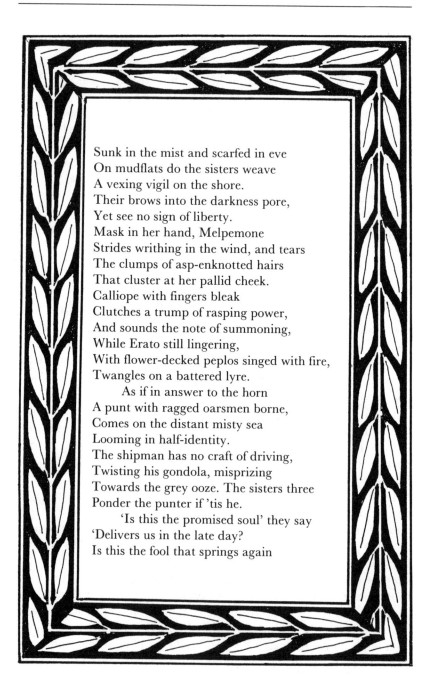

Sunk in the mist and scarfed in eve
On mudflats do the sisters weave
A vexing vigil on the shore.
Their brows into the darkness pore,
Yet see no sign of liberty.
Mask in her hand, Melpemone
Strides writhing in the wind, and tears
The clumps of asp-enknotted hairs
That cluster at her pallid cheek.
Calliope with fingers bleak
Clutches a trump of rasping power,
And sounds the note of summoning,
While Erato still lingering,
With flower-decked peplos singed with fire,
Twangles on a battered lyre.
　　　As if in answer to the horn
A punt with ragged oarsmen borne,
Comes on the distant misty sea
Looming in half-identity.
The shipman has no craft of driving,
Twisting his gondola, misprizing
Towards the grey ooze. The sisters three
Ponder the punter if 'tis he.
　　　'Is this the promised soul' they say
'Delivers us in the late day?
Is this the fool that springs again

The Muses to the world of men?'
    Yet the man rolls with ragged thrusting
All the oily waves mistrusting,
And through the mirk the polesmen comes
And stares upon the three fair ones,
A fearful face upon the fog.
    'This is some educated dog,'
They cry at last, 'with eager snout
Sniffing his own position out.
Blind is his eye and deaf his lugs,
His lips too prim for Muses' dugs.
How shall we tip him in the lake?'
    But still the punter waves his wake
Slicing down the rushes raw,
And grounds upon the nether shore.
    Sudden he is gone. Another
Worried-faced and elder brother
Comes to peer across the mere.
He, it seems, has less to fear,
For with fingers quivering
He breaks the air of Hades dim,
And a hand across the night
Thrusts towards the spirits bright,
Though laughing do the sisters spy it.
    'Look,' say the sprightly ones 'Let's lie it
Under our feet and mud it flat.'

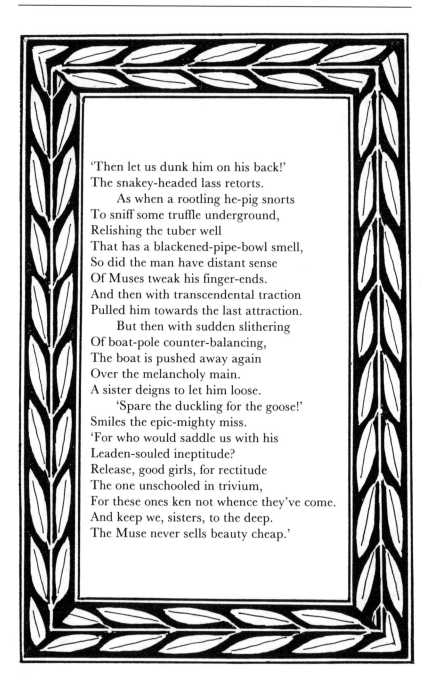

'Then let us dunk him on his back!'
The snakey-headed lass retorts.
    As when a rootling he-pig snorts
To sniff some truffle underground,
Relishing the tuber well
That has a blackened-pipe-bowl smell,
So did the man have distant sense
Of Muses tweak his finger-ends.
And then with transcendental traction
Pulled him towards the last attraction.
    But then with sudden slithering
Of boat-pole counter-balancing,
The boat is pushed away again
Over the melancholy main.
A sister deigns to let him loose.
    'Spare the duckling for the goose!'
Smiles the epic-mighty miss.
'For who would saddle us with his
Leaden-souled ineptitude?
Release, good girls, for rectitude
The one unschooled in trivium,
For these ones ken not whence they've come.
And keep we, sisters, to the deep.
The Muse never sells beauty cheap.'

But once he pedalled on Foxview Road, O'Ryan's optimism seemed to begin to decline. There was, he sensed, a fateful change in things, even on the southern slopes of Oxford, which were not immune to the changes of the city. For what had happened down the hill was not a freak occurrence: a pattern had been set, and he dreaded its further showings. O'Ryan then began wearily to revolve the irrationality of what had happened, and try to ascertain with some light of reason what the situation now was. *His* Dr Alting was not Dr Alting. It would have been odd for Snare to recommend a man of *his* convictions! Yet *his* Dr Alting had not contradicted his being called Dr Alting — if indeed O'Ryan had actually called him in his presence by his presumed name. But then again *his* Dr Alting had signed himself so in his letter. He must *be* Dr Alting. But there must be *two* Dr Altings. But if there were tw . . .

O'Ryan tailed off, for he had come to the gate of the house, and at once he sensed that the house had been disturbed. In the mist he could see great scars of broken wood on the gate itself, as though some big vehicle had scraped the rotten timber off when it went by. Then as he approached, he saw the driveway torn up by giant tyre-tracks, and the weed-tumbled lawn churned into raw, frosty earth. When he came to the house itself he saw great scraping marks over its porch floor, oil-stains on the door, loose boxes and scattered straw and packing-foam in the garden. It was as though a fair had been recently set up in the grounds, and had hastily vamoosed.

O'Ryan feeling doomed by these sights, parked his bike in the spot he used before, went up to the porch and rang the bell. No sound came. He rang again. The muffled cow-bell noise was gone. Something must have broken the old mechanism. O'Ryan did not like to imitate a barbarian, or intrude any hysterical emotionalism into the calm of *his* Dr Alting's world, but he felt he had to get his attention somehow. So he knocked on the door. The house echoed hollowly. Somehow the quality of the noise was forlorn and seemed to suggest that all human beings, if not all objects in the house, had left. He went up to the door and tried to peer through the mottled glass. It seemed as if there were nothing now in the hall.

He dashed across to his left, and tried to peer in the window of the room he had not before visited, but which could have been a dining room. He saw that it was empty. The walls were vacant. There was no furniture in it at all, just bare boards, not even a carpet. This was very strange. But perhaps it was like that anyway. He then thought of the parlour where he had been shown in before, and dashed across to the right of the porch. Peering through the dust of the window, he found to his dismay that the curtains had been drawn. Why should they draw the curtains like that? Something had happened! Something bad had happened to Dr Alting.

Dr Alting! What Dr Alting? O'Ryan felt sick. The thought he had been doing his best to avoid: what Dr Alting? came suddenly and unavoidably now he was in his region, and forced itself on his consciousness. What Dr Alting? He had never allowed himself to consider this, because of all the puzzles which had baffled him in recent times, this was the one question he did not want answered. What Dr Alting? There was no Dr Alting. There was nobody living in this house. It was empty. It had been empty too on Tuesday and he had dreamed everything. He had been to a phantom-tutorial. It could only be so. It was all too complete, too perfect to be real!

So O'Ryan sombrely went to the door again, and tried the handle. The door was locked, the handle turned in vain. He walked around the outside of the house, looking for an open window. They all seemed to be secured and unyielding. He passed along the side of the mansion, and threaded his way through the weeds, and the still-yellow sunflowers to the back. Here he saw in the mist the lovely overgrown world he had looked at before, both from his tutor's window and from Miss Alting's. The figs and apple-trees were dropping their fruit, littering the ground with decaying riches. In the clustering dusk the faint gold sunflowers smelt of seeds and decay, and the foggy frost suspended everything in decline.

O'Ryan passed round to the back of the house. The windows all looked bleak. He had never seen the house from this side. He went up to the conservatory. He tried the door. It was not locked. He entered into the house with a thudding heart. Would there be warmth and companionship? Would they smile and say all was well? The house at once seemed sombre and hopeless. The conservatory itself was empty, no wrought-iron chairs, no stand, no plants. He went into the house and saw the room on his right was empty. He pushed the door and went into the study. The room was dead. Its walls were dull. His footsteps echoed, as at the end of things. The chair was gone where his tutor had sat, the ornaments, the tables. The bookshelves lay raw and vacant, bleak, stripped, bereft. The fire was quenched, dusty the embers. There was no comfort here. Gone were the sounds of poetry.

O'Ryan suddenly thought of Miss Alting. He dashed out and up the stairs. He rushed into her room, bursting open the door. The room was empty. Only the bed, the great bed remained, with its mattress bare of covers, askew on bare boards in the fading light. All was dull, lost, echoing, barren, drear, forlorn. O'Ryan stood still and frowned in pain. He went softly to the bed, placed his hands together as if praying and sat down. Then he keeled over, his head on the pillow, and wept.

The mist hung all about the house. November was nearly gone. The term was ending in fog and cold. A hardly noticed dusk came down, gloomily netting all the woods, softly pocketing all in its woolly overcoat. Deeper and deeper sunk the night. O'Ryan lay there weeping. How far, how far away was happiness!

But then he heard a car approaching. It was crunching up the gravel in the drive. Dr Alting had returned! He leapt up and ran to see. Headlights were swirling in the passage, throwing beams over the ceiling. O'Ryan at the window saw a car down on the drive, and a man get out, an old man. He was fumbling in his pocket for the key. O'Ryan was sure it was him. He sensed it was a friend. O'Ryan hurried down the stairs.

'Dr Alting?' he called as the door opened.

'Who's that?' said a voice, and a torch dazzled O'Ryan, as the old man peered into the darkness.

'Dr Alting, is that you?'

'Who is that?' The old man approached. 'Why,' he said surprised, 'it's Mr O'Ryan!'

'Dr Alting? It's not you then?' O'Ryan held his hands before his eyes. He stopped to sniff and hurriedly wipe away his tears.

'It's Sir Walter Lawrence,' said the voice. 'The President of your college, who, as this house is college property, has some right to be here. And some little amazement therefore at seeing *you* here,

Mr O'Ryan. Just as he has some amazement at seeing the house in such a state.'

'You mean empty?' said O'Ryan. 'That's what has astonished me! How on earth does it come to be empty?'

'Hm,' said Sir Walter moving into the parlour. 'A question to be asked. But why *are* you here?' Sir Walter came out again.

'I came to see Dr Alting,' said O'Ryan. 'God knows what can have happened to him. I'm desperate to find him, in fact. My whole career depends on it. You know I'm supposed to come and see you on Monday at four, so you can tell me I've been sent down. Well, Dr Alting is the one man who can save me from that, the one man who can testify that I really *did* come to a tutorial with him. But when I come here to ask him to vouch for me, what do I find: he's gone, there's no sign of him, and the house is empty! It's all just a bloody nightmare! It really is!' O'Ryan sighed and stood there thoroughly tearful.

'Hm,' said Sir Walter. 'Let's go and talk in one of the rooms. We can sit on the floor if there are really no chairs. I am finding all this rather depressing.'

He led the way into the study, and drew O'Ryan to the window, where they both then sat down in the fading light. Sir Walter set his torch on its end, so that it shone on the ceiling. They sat beneath its banded chandelier.

'Why do you speak as though you think Dr Alting lives here?' said Sir Walter.

'Because he does,' said O'Ryan. 'I came to my tutorial here on Tuesday. I sat with him talking in this very room. I know Dr Snare disputes this, and says that Dr Alting also denies it. But I know I was here, and this room was furnished. It's completely untrue to say that I missed this tutorial. I've got the essay I did and the question for next week. I'm being sent down unjustly. I was going to tell you this on Monday at four. I was here. I had a tutorial, and this place was furnished.'

'Oh yes, certainly it was furnished,' said Sir Walter. 'I saw it myself. And I rather wanted to look again at some of the books.'

'You've seen it yourself? Did you visit Dr Alting?'

'Er — no. No, I just came to see the house,' smiled Sir Walter. 'And I rather think that Dr Alting lives in Iffley.'

'No,' said O'Ryan. 'He was here, he and his daughter, Miss

Alting. She has the room just above this.'

'Dr Alting has no daughter.'

'That's what Snare said. Come to think of it . . .' O'Ryan sighed, 'that's what Dr Alting said too. Sir Walter, please don't send me down. Send me to a psychiatrist, if you will. But I really did come here and have a tute with somebody!'

Sir Walter looked over towards him. 'What was it made you come here to see Dr Alting?'

'I had a letter,' O'Ryan fumbled in his pocket. 'No, I must have left it in my digs. But I had a letter from Dr Alting telling me to come here. He said with his daughter sick, as she is, he couldn't come down to the college, but would see me at eleven here in his house instead.'

'Have you retained this letter?'

'Oh yes.'

'Then perhaps you will bring the letter with you, when you come to see me on Monday.'

'Yes, of course.'

'It would be evidence, would it not, of your good faith? It might well furnish the proof that could enable me to revise the decision concerning your dismissal.'

O'Ryan swallowed.

'Can you describe Dr Alting to me?' said Sir Walter.

'Yes,' said O'Ryan, 'with vigour and pleasure. He had a big head, leonine, and a shock of white hair, kindly eyes, a big deep voice, and a quizzical half-raised eyebrow that gave him a comic or satiric look. He was blind.'

'Blind!' said Sir Walter.

'Blind, and his daughter was dumb.'

There was a long pause.

'Mr O'Ryan,' sighed Sir Walter, 'has anyone ever told you that you don't make it easy for yourself by your forthright and unguarded way of speaking? I would recommend that you hasten the necessary ageing process of life by circumspection before it is too late. You have given me a very interesting description. It certainly seems real, and not unlike someone connected with this house. I only wonder how you could have seen any such thing.' Sir Walter sighed and looked about the derelict room. 'And what purpose is served by its now being so bleak and deserted.'

'You can't know,' sighed O'Ryan, 'how lonely it is here now. All the spirit of the place seems to have gone. Before, it was inhabited by beauty and strength and power. Now it is dead. I can't believe how all this is departed!'

'Ah.'

'There was such happiness here, and love. And Dr Alting told me so many things! They were the very secrets my mind craved for.' O'Ryan smiled. 'Only one thing he didn't tell me, though: the explanation of a dream I had had, a strange dream of Eighteenth Century ballrooms, and visions of dwarves and giants.'

'Dwarves and giants? He spoke of that?'

'Oh yes! — No, I mean no.' O'Ryan smiled. 'But everything else he told me. All I needed to set me on the path. How to work and develop. A tutorial setting work for a lifetime's study.'

Sir Walter was silent for a long time. But then he decided he must speak. 'You see, Mr O'Ryan, since this house is owned by the college, as President I came a few weeks ago to look it over, and found it furnished, stacked high in fact, but in an unkempt and untidy state, so that I decided we ought at least to try and tidy it. I contacted a postgraduate student of mine, a Mr Bergson, whom I supervise in his studies in German history, and he agreed to come with some students and clean it. I have been assured that the cleaning was carried out. But it seems that thereafter a far more drastic purgative operation was put in force, about which I am not altogether satisfied.'

O'Ryan was staring at the President with amazement on his face. But before he could speak, Sir Walter continued.

'You see, Mr O'Ryan, long ago this house used to belong to an old Classics don of St Mary's. He was really quite famous — maybe you've heard of him? Professor Maeonides. He was Professor of Classics and Greek Literature. He specialised in a type of structural analysis, Proportional Synopsis, which he had invented, and by which he revealed the beauty of classic proportions. Just recently, becoming interested in the property which he left to the college, I have been reading both about him and from his works. In his book *Return*, which was published around the time of the War, he outlined a scheme of most unusual perspicuity, which demonstrated how modern culture could be set back on what he considered to be its proper traditional and Classical tracks.

'Maeonides held the view that modern art in pursuing constant rebellion had lost both its skills and its soul. These skills and this soul were manifest everywhere in the modern world, and yet were totally shunned by its effete culture. According to him, the modern world is in all respects the product of the Renaissance, in that its finance, its technology, its science, its globalism, all originated with that movement. Yet while the modern world is Renaissance, and therefore based on Classicism and Reason, its culture is in no way relevant to or reflective of this. The culture of the modern world is based on rebellion against such values and is therefore pitted against the society that supports it. This subversiveness he sees as typical of modern art and as stemming from the cult of Romanticism.

'In the Eighteenth Century, which was the last great age of Classicism, the masculine spirit of the time infused the pursuit of science. The arts meanwhile reacted against this relentless pursuit of reason, and fell into various sorts of — what he called — feminine indulgence. Romanticism and Socialist Realism he regarded as aberrations from the natural masculine traditions of Western Civilisation, and when Romantic cults such as those of rebellion, proletarianism, savagery and egotism became dominant, culture was on a path towards degradation.

'Maeonides claimed that although the liberating urge of Romanticism produced some great artistic masterpieces, it was only during the period while the arts continued to respect the old forms that their products wielded any power. As time went by the constant rebellion continually degraded culture, until skills became lost to the point of extinction in modern art. Maeonides claimed that as the arts declined, their influence declined also, until at present they hold only a peripheral place in society. All this artistic degradation he regarded as unfortunate, crass and effete, but ultimately of no serious effect. It was in philosophy, however, that he claimed the influence of Romanticism had had the most catastrophic results.

'While in the Nineteenth Century the cult of Reason continued to be the basis for progress in science and technology, philosophy was invaded by the feminine cult of Romanticism, where it produced monsters of speculation. In the realms of ethical and political philosophy, this movement ultimately produced the pernicious creeds of Fascism and Communism. Romantic cults of the superman, and the notion that great men are above morals, led to the excesses of the former. Romantic cults of revolution and of the supremacy of the proletariat promoted the various revolutions of the latter. Maeonides thought these cults were to blame for the wars and purges of the Twentieth Century, and he characterised them as the codes of dwarves and giants.

'I fear Mr O'Ryan, that you have either been the victim of some practical joke, or else have tapped some spiritual force emanating from this house. I will say, however, that I believe you in your account of your tutorial adventure, for there can be no other satisfactory explanation as to why you are here. If you can produce Dr Alting's letter, perhaps we can settle the matter. It is plain that you have come hither by bicycle. It would be superfluous to offer you a lift back to town. We shall meet anyway on Monday at four in my office, after I have had a chance of consulting Dr Snare.'

The President fixed O'Ryan with a look. 'I think, Mr O'Ryan, you would find Maeonides's books of great interest.'

Chapter Eight

W hen seasons change, the world at first shivers in delight, as at a breeze from the region of romance. But when change holds, the old order boils up in stormy outrage, hail teems from the clouds, winter winds gnaw at the sand-dunes. The spirits of season, settling in, are assailed by the faltering passés, and in rich turmoil the ghosts caper in glee.

In rage thus at a new impostor, the old winds stored in the west, on Cotswold hills pounced in the cyclone. The willows of Windrush flattened in awe. The benighted cattle turned their backs, the woods of Wytham bounced and tumbled to the buffets. Then flapping the night air over Oxford the twigs of beeches flew, slabs of roof and greenhouse crashed over houses. Dust-bin lids went madly cantering down leaf-streaming Banbury Road, and the oaks howled out over Port Meadow. Wild even along the station platforms of stolid British Rail clattered the pelting cavalry of bottles and cans. In the night of gales came the spirits. The ghosts rose up in the city. And the otherworld girls trooped about the streets.

* * * *

'I seem to have two engagements for four o'clock today,' said Sir Walter to his secretary, as she waited in his office. 'I had forgotten that the Estates Committee was meeting at four o'clock. How did we get into this mix-up?'

'Ah,' she said, 'Well, I did think it odd, but Dr Snare made this appointment for you. I pointed out to him there would be a clash. But then Dr Fobey, who happened to come into the office with Dr

Snare said as Estates Committee chairman he could assure me that there wouldn't be any objections. You could be late going to the meeting, and it wouldn't really cause any problems. They also moved the meeting forward by a quarter of an hour.'

The President studied his desk. Then he looked at his watch and said, 'Could you phone Dr Snare, and ask him to come and see me straight away? I don't think he is teaching just now.'

'Of course,' said the secretary and left, shutting the door very quietly.

The President picked up his pen, from his Florentine holder selected a page of note-paper, and wrote calmly and in a rapid hand. Having finished the brief note he studied it, folded it into an envelope, addressed it, and rose from his chair.

When he came out to the secretary's office, she was just putting the phone down.

'Dr Snare is coming right over,' she smiled.

'Good,' said the President. 'If I mind the office, could you just pop this round to the porter's lodge? I'd like this to be there straight away.'

The secretary took the note politely, gave a quick glance at the name of its addressee, put on her raincoat and left.

Sir Walter went back into his room. He pulled over a file marked *Maeonides House*, and opening it, pondered its contents. He had left the door of the secretary's office open, and so after reading for a while he did not miss Snare's approach.

'Come in, Dr Snare,' he called without looking up.

Snare came forward curiously, forming his lips into many shapes. He was not sure how to react to being summoned in this headmasterly fashion. He considered that Dr Lawrence was treating him to a display of earnest reading. Quietly he decided not to put up with it.

'You wanted to see me,' he said, interrupting the President's study.

Sir Walter looked up. 'Yes, I see I've got an appointment made to see O'Ryan again. And I saw from your note that you and the Senior Tutor have sent him down.'

'Oh yes,' said Snare. 'I'm afraid this is so. I've seen him myself and told him the news. I just thought it would be best if you could formalise his dismissal.'

'Why at four o' clock?' smiled the President. 'I have an Estates Committee meeting then.'

'Dr Fobey told me it would be convenient.'

'Not as convenient as three o' clock. Why do you think I should send O'Ryan down?'

'He has already been told he has been sent down,' said Snare precisely. 'While you were away, he missed his tutorial at the first possible opportunity. I have a note from Dr Alting complaining about this. It was highly discourteous, confrontational, irresponsible and went flatly against what you had told him. There is no alternative but to send him down.'

'Yet I understand I have the last word on this?'

'I think the Senior Tutor is the important one here,' said Snare. 'He has agreed to send down O'Ryan. O'Ryan *has* been sent down. You see, Sir Walter, I think you must realise that unlike the diplomatic service, an Oxford college is a democratic institution. A college is governed by its fellows. The fellows act in a body, and you are merely first among equals.'

'And the college fellows as a whole have decided that O'Ryan is to be sent down? What meeting was this? Why was I not present?'

'The decision has been taken democratically by the Senior Tutor and myself, since we are the fellows involved.'

'But have you consulted with any one else?'

Snare gave an elaborate sigh. 'Sir Walter,' he said, 'I don't need to. But if you like, I can ask many of the fellows this afternoon at the Estates Committee meeting.'

'The Estates Committee meeting? I never realised you were on the Estates Committee.'

'Dr Fobey has just co-opted me. I'm to give a report on the books from the Maeonides house.'

'Ah, then you were involved in their removal?'

'No, that was Dr Fobey's work as chairman.'

'And since he was the fellow involved, did he also perhaps take a one-man democratic decision?'

Snare sighed. 'I can't answer for Dr Fobey.'

'Well, thank you,' said the President. 'I will let you know of my meeting with Mr O'Ryan, and inform you of whether or not I dismiss him. I'll see you all at the committee meeting.'

'Er — yes.' Snare smiled, then looked hesitant. 'But you'll be half an hour or three quarters of an hour late.'

'That seems to be the arrangement,' shrugged he.

The secretary had returned from the porter's lodge.

'I think I better go,' said Snare.

Sir Walter nodded.

*   *   *   *

O'Ryan was busily searching through his papers yet again, but still he could not find it. It was three o' clock and he saw the President at four. Where was it? Once more he took the folder with his essays, that of his reading notes, and his wafer-thin envelope of his lecture notes, and placing them out on his bed, counted them over elaborately, just to make sure he had got everything there.

He then went through them page by page. His quarry could not be found. It did not lurk among his own handwritten essays. There was nothing of a different order among his photocopied pages, or his notes, hurried, irregular and illegible, and there was certainly nothing among all three pages of lecture notes — the material on which O'Ryan based his analysis of the English Faculty.

His briefcase he attacked again. In it he found sweet-papers, handouts, club programmes, letters from other students, college magazines and a half-sucked lollipop coated in fluff. Of a precious typewritten letter re-arranging his tutorial venue and sent from the assumed home of a Dr Alting there was no sign. O'Ryan sighed, stared frustratedly at the mess on his bed, and then for a final time went over to his desk.

The top of the desk he searched, lifting up each knick-knack, each of the two invitations, each book from St Mary's or the English Faculty Library to flip through the pages in a fanlike fashion that puffed up the hair over his face, and made his tangled black locks dance in exasperation. All around the desk he studied once more, scraping about on the dusty floor, and looked again at the hamburger cartons thrown in his wastepaper-basket. He finally opened the drawer of his desk, and went through the brochures and souvenir programmes, page by page searching their polished colours. Dr Alting's letter was nowhere to be seen.

He certainly hadn't thrown it away. Something had happened to it.

O'Ryan was sure that it had been there the day before, or at least the day before that. He knew well the place he kept it. It was stacked with the two invitations under the statuette of Thoth, the Egyptian god of literature. Thoth was painted green and yellow, held the overall shape of an ibis and was from a tourist shop probed on a school-trip to Luxor. It grasped in its feet important missives. But Thoth had for some reason seen fit to let this important charge go. O'Ryan could not think what had happened to it. He slumped his arms on the flat of his desk, set his chin on his hand and stared despairingly into space.

O'Ryan agreed with everyone that there were times when it seemed impossible to win, and he conceded that this might be just one of them. He analysed fairly that the situation might merely be an ordinary part of the glorious cussedness of life's complications. Yet the way things at present were seemingly happening so frequently to thwart his progress was — even allowing for the cussed syndrome — unaccountable. There seemed to be some sort of Fate that seemed to be malign working against him. How else could he, O'Ryan, have got into these scrapes? He, O'Ryan, was not born to fail. He had a lucky face. Till now he had always fallen on its pair of opposites. What purpose was being served by this continual thrusting down? He felt like one of the barrators in Dante's Malbowge Number Five.

Noises of voices came on the stairs as a group of students raced up to one of the rooms opposite O'Ryan's. Suddenly he had an idea. Fosdyke might have pinched it. Fosdyke was part of the gang who were so interested in his phantom-tutorial! He remembered how the President had said Bergson was a postgraduate student of his, and it was true that Bergson was doing research into modern German history. What if the gang were part of the mob who were up cleaning Foxview Road, and then had plotted an elaborate joke together? Maybe they wanted him to go there, and get stuck at an empty house. And then had stolen the incriminating letter? But —

The voices had gone into Fosdyke's room, so he must be there. O'Ryan went in his room to see.

'Ah, the born poet!' cried Ramsey, as he lolled on the bed, while Fosdyke attended a coffee-jar in the corner.

'Listen, you lot,' said O'Ryan with a thoughtful frown, 'have you been on any errands with Bergson of late?'

'Errands, what sort of errands?' said Ramsey cheerily.

'Well, jobs — manual jobs for instance.'

'Oh!' shrieked Mansfield, who was not usually with the group, 'heaven forfend we should undertake manual labour!'

'Well, you wouldn't, Mansfield: you have your nails to protect. But these others might.'

'Well, I haven't,' shrugged Ramsey.

'Want a mug of coffee, O'Ryan?' said Fosdyke with the familiar flatness with which flat-mates are addressed.

'No,' said O'Ryan, looking at his watch. 'I've got to go into town soon. But listen,' he frowned again, 'you haven't knicked anything from my room, have you?'

'Good Lord!' exclaimed Mansfield, 'he's accusing you of pilfering now! What sort of a barbarian do you live with here?'

'Just shut up, will you?' said O'Ryan. 'Something's gone from my room, and I want to know if any of you have seen it.'

'Well, what it is?'

'A letter.'

'Oh, say no more!' guffawed Mansfield, 'no wonder he's so touchy, if it's a billet-doux!''

'Well, it isn't a billet-doux. It was a letter from my tutor rearranging the venue of a tutorial.'

O'Ryan noticed that Fosdyke took a long time making the coffee, but that Ramsey was staring at him rather white-faced.

'Come on: have you pinched it, Ramsey?'

'No, honestly, O'Ryan,' he replied. 'When could I have pinched it? I've only just got here.'

'Well, what about yesterday?'

'But I wasn't here yesterday.'

'Fosdyke was.'

'Fuck it, I live here.'

'So who else was here?'

'Bergson?' said Ramsey.

'No, he wasn't!' said Fosdyke. 'Look, what is all this? Is this about your phantom-tutorial?' Fosdyke stood up now and handed the coffee out to Ramsey and the now-silenced Mansfield. He kept his standing position. 'You're the one who claims that you had a tutorial up in Boar's Hill, O'Ryan. We've always maintained that you were fantasising. Now it seems you're accusing us of stealing something to do with your fantasy. I think that's going a bit far.'

'So do I,' said O'Ryan. 'A joke's a joke, but I reckon you've all gone quite far enough.'

The phone rang on the landing downstairs.

'I'll get it!' said Fosdyke quickly, dashed out and thundered down the stairs.

As his voice was heard talking muffled below, Ramsey looked at O'Ryan and shrugged. 'Honestly,' he said, 'I know nothing about this letter being pinched.' He paused. 'But Bergson was here yesterday.'

'And has there been some sort of joke played on me?' said O'Ryan.

'Well, may be,' said Ramsey. 'But you've joined in it too.'

'What do you mean?'

'Well, all this talk about having a tutorial! You know damn well you made all that up!'

O'Ryan stared puzzled at Ramsey, as Mansfield stared puzzled at them both.

'It's for you,' said Fosdyke's voice coming up the stairs.

'Oh?' said O'Ryan. 'Christ! It's Monday! It isn't the President?'

'No,' said Fosdyke with a sneer, 'why should it be? I suppose you'll be astonished to hear that it's an old man who calls himself Dr Alting.' He smirked unpleasantly. 'Nicely timed, O'Ryan! You keep it up well!'

O'Ryan was completely baffled. Then his spirits rose with a great bound, and he leapt out of the door and careered down the stairs.

'Hullo, is that Dr Alting?' he cried excitedly.

'Yes,' said the deep and kindly voice. 'Mr O'Ryan, I'm glad I've caught you. I've got some urgent but happy news. I wonder if you could come up and see me?'

'Certainly!' said O'Ryan. 'I'd love to! When?'

'Why,' said Dr Alting, 'now, as soon as you can. In fact any time today before four-thirty. After that, I'm afraid, it will be too late. You see, my daughter and I are —'

'What, four-thirty *today*?' exclaimed O'Ryan.

'Yes. Can you not make it?'

O'Ryan paused. 'But why? I mean: four-thirty today?'

'I'm afraid so. We are leaving, you see, Mr O'Ryan, and at four-thirty our friends are coming to pick us up. We are going to —'

'You're leaving? What, leaving Oxford?'

'I'm sorry about this, Mr O'Ryan. It will mean I cannot offer you another tutorial. It has all just happened since we last met. We have had the news from the States that there is hope of a cure for my daughter, and they want her to come for treatment straight away. The amazing thing is that she has made remarkable improvements of late. You must come and see her. You will be astonished.'

There was a pause.

'Mr O'Ryan, are you all right?'

'No,' moaned O'Ryan. 'I'm desolated! I want to see you both more than anything in the world! But I can't come now. I really can't. I have to go and see the President of St Mary's at four. I couldn't get up to Boar's Hill and down again in time for that. And if I do see the President, then I won't be finished in time to get up and see you both before four-thirty. The meeting with the President is very urgent. Things are bad enough as it is. But if I don't show, it will mean he will send me down. I may get sent down in any case. You see —'

'I see! Then you can't possibly come. You must not risk your future, Mr O'Ryan. How sad!' Dr Alting paused. 'But never mind. No doubt we shall meet again, when my daughter has had her treatment. I'm sorry that I shall not be able to give you another tutorial. We got on so well, and my daughter was especially cheered to meet you. She was so looking forward to seeing you again. She wanted to tell you something about your name. Just a little foolery. She —'

'Tell her I'll be there,' said O'Ryan. 'Allow me about twenty minutes. I'll come up on my bike right now. I'll get down again in time to see the President. I can do it. Don't worry. But I really must see you both. I have so many things to ask you.'

'Well, that would be wonderful!' sighed Dr Alting. 'But do be sure it's all right. And if by any chance I don't answer the door, just come in and go straight up to my daughter's room.'

'Right — Oh, Dr Alting,' O'Ryan hurriedly spoke into the phone, 'just in case anything goes wrong, please let me ask you this. It's about —' There was a click, and the phone went dead 'what has happened to . . . Dr Alting?' O'Ryan paused.

Then he ran.

*   *   *   *

Heavy clouds were over the town. The weather had changed again. The winds had died and the sky threatened a frosty deluge. The streets grew quiet. A few students, fleeing the grey-banked tempest, were clutching their coats, as they pressed towards warm doors. Rooks looked up at the cindery sky and jumped towards deeper branches. The roe-deer clustered to the sheltering wall.

The spirits were meeting. Three female forms stood among books and shelves: one with a mask, one with a glass, and one with a clock. They watched by the table of the SCR library. Before them lay the papers from the house. There were the poems illustrated by Miss Alting. They looked at the gloomy, black door on the page and gazed deep into the ink. They saw, among visions of the world beyond . . .

*   *   *   *

'And apologies from the President also,' said the secretary, putting down her notes.

The others in the committee room looked slightly puzzled, and then gazed at Dr Fobey, who was white-faced and highly nervous.

'I'm altering the order of the agenda,' he blurted, his cheeks working neurotically. 'I want to kill this matter of the Holywell Quad straightaway! The newsletters to the alumni are ready to go out, and we must appeal to our old members for the modern quad. Quick show of hands then, if you please!'

'But shouldn't we wait for the President?' said an earnest voice.

'We haven't got time!' said Fobey. 'He's voting for the Hammerstein anyway. He told me. And we don't need his vote to carry it.'

'On the subject of the President,' said a leisurely voice, 'I would just like to say publicly, while we have the chance here in his

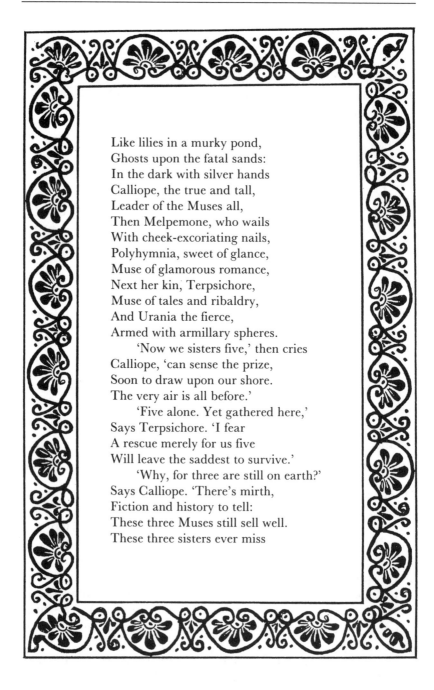

Like lilies in a murky pond,
Ghosts upon the fatal sands:
In the dark with silver hands
Calliope, the true and tall,
Leader of the Muses all,
Then Melpemone, who wails
With cheek-excoriating nails,
Polyhymnia, sweet of glance,
Muse of glamorous romance,
Next her kin, Terpsichore,
Muse of tales and ribaldry,
And Urania the fierce,
Armed with armillary spheres.
     'Now we sisters five,' then cries
Calliope, 'can sense the prize,
Soon to draw upon our shore.
The very air is all before.'
     'Five alone. Yet gathered here,'
Says Terpsichore. 'I fear
A rescue merely for us five
Will leave the saddest to survive.'
     'Why, for three are still on earth?'
Says Calliope. 'There's mirth,
Fiction and history to tell:
These three Muses still sell well.
These three sisters ever miss

Our gloomy right to shine in Dis,
Our treat in ancient scholar's boudoir
Merely to haunt the odd intruder.
They bask in modernity!
Who are we to weep those three?'
    'Three and five are only eight.'
    'For the further you must wait!'
Calliope replies. 'But see:
Come not of liberty the three?'
    Deep upon the dark horizon
With their decagynous eyes on,
Three shapes float with hurried craft
Born on a sail-entattered raft.
    'Ay, our living sisters near!'
The others cry. 'See at the rear,
Sails Euterpe, queen of novels,
Scanning her poor comrades' hovels.
And — what a nose! — is that the Muse
Thalia, with her baggy trouse?
And see we the grave face of Clio?
Is it? Hail, you handsome trio!
Never have more welcome ladies
Paddled the glum lake of Hades!'
    Quick now from the ship also
The ghost-girls wave and call hullo!
The diamond-studded, grave and masked,

Shaking unsteadily the craft.
　　　'Living Muses, loving hail!'
Call the Hell-girls. 'Furl your sail.
Come, let us clip you, each and all!
　　　'Sisters dear!' the earthlings call.
'Waste no embraces, but step well:
Board our barque, and let's pell-mell!
For up above with flips and fun
We have enchantments to be done!
A learned city, sunk in slumber,
Is to be magicked into wonder!
Nine of us to make the spell.
There's no time to lose in Hell.'
　　　The sisters board. The world to wake
They speed across the infernal lake.

absence, that I can't help feeling we seem to be giving him the impression that he is not really needed. I agree we had to make it clear from the outset — as we all planned — that the President is not the dictator of college policy, but I feel we may have been —'

'We can't talk about this now,' said Fobey, shuddering with nerves. His staring eyes and white face made him look distinctly deranged.

'I'm sorry,' continued the voice, 'but I think we should. It is all rather absurd if the fellows of the President's own college treat him as a kind of slightly pointless mascot.'

'Oh, I don't think we think this for a moment!' came an indignant voice backed up by a lot of affronted murmurs.

'Will you all kindly shut up!' said Fobey with hysteria in his voice. 'We will proceed to the vote on the Holywell Quad at once.'

'No, we won't,' said the more stern voice of Hapgood. 'I don't think this committee can proceed at all, until we have an explanation of why Dr Snare is here. He is not a member of the committee, and I fail to see why he should be privy to its deliberations.'

Fobey glared at him. 'I have asked Dr Snare to come along to the committee, since he is, as you know, a very distinguished English Literature critic, whose advice I have sought over the disposal of the Maeonides library. He has recently been in a position to examine the books, and he has a short report to give to us, for which purpose I have exercised my power as chairman to co-opt him onto the committee, and he will remain a co-opted member for the rest of this term.'

'Does this mean he can vote on the quad?'

Fobey looked hunted, then rallied and put on a baffled expression. 'Well, I hadn't really considered the matter.'

The atmosphere in the room chilled.

The earnest Mr Hapgood became grim. 'Have you spoken to him of the quad before?'

Fobey blustered, 'I dare say we have discussed it. It has been a common talking point in the SCR.'

'Is he voting your way?'

Fobey was incensed. 'Just what are you suggesting?'

'Look, I'm in favour of the Hammerstein quad just as you are, but I don't think we are doing the case any good if we are seen to be packing the committee!'

The indignant voice trumpeted, 'Well, really! I'm sure such a thought was far from the mind of Dr Fobey!' but the voice was not supported this time by any murmurs of agreement.

Fobey looked as though he was going to crack. His beady eyes went quickly round the room. He jumped in. 'Can we have a quick show of hands as to how fellows would vote on the question of the Holywell Quad? Those in favour of the old-style design by Quintin Hargreaves?'

The air was tense, as fellows began putting up their hands.

Dr Fobey remained stiff. 'I make that six, Secretary.'

'Yes,' said the secretary. 'I make that six.'

'Write it down!' said Fobey. 'And now for the modern design of Mr Hammerstein whom we all met at the guest-night not so very long ago?'

The silence was sharp. Hands began to rise. Fobey and the secretary counted them.

'I make that seven, Secretary, including my own, of course.'

'Yes indeed.'

'And you are abstaining, Mr Davenport?'

'No, I'm undecided.'

'You've no business to be undecided! Will you kindly vote? You have had ample warning of this!'

Davenport looked at his agenda. 'I'm not sure that what you say is correct,' he said. 'If you notice, the agenda has the vote on the Holywell Quad last. Before that we have matters such as the Maeonides house to consider, and the report on the repairs to the tower. Also the President is supposed to be here. For myself, I intended to listen to what was said during the meeting as advertised and then make up my mind. That I still intend to do.'

'The President is not coming,' said Fobey, boiling over in rage. 'It's pointless waiting for him. Really, I've had a great deal of trouble with this already, and I can't put up with this any more! Will you please vote? The President doesn't have any say in this!'

'I do beg all your pardon for being a few minutes late,' said Sir Walter smoothly, as he stunned Fobey by entering behind him. 'But while I was away I seemed to have acquired some bilocatory bookings, which has necessitated a rearrangement. I am in good time, I hope, for the important matters at the end of the agenda?'

Fobey had closed his eyes and was wiping his face with his handkerchief.

*   *   *   *

Clanging onto the railings outside St Mary's O'Ryan left his bicycle without bothering to lock it, and dashed into the college, bearing a letter in his hand round the front quad, through the arch and up to the door of the President's office. Taking a deep breath he swung open the door of the little ante-room, and found the secretary's office open, which he entered.

There was nobody there. He looked all round, but although an empty tea-cup stood on her desk, there was no secretary behind it. Knowing he had no time to waste, O'Ryan knocked on the door of the President himself. There was no answer. With even greater audacity, he then opened it.

The room was empty.

'Can I help you?' came a voice.

O'Ryan spun round and saw one of the secretaries from the Bursar's office staring in at him.

'I'm looking for the President,' said O'Ryan.

'I can see that,' she said. 'But I'm afraid he's in a meeting.'

'Ah, but he's due to see me at four.'

'Is he?'

'Yes, but I can't make it. I have to dash off on some business which he and I were recently talking about. He'll understand, but I need to tell him. I've written it all down here in a letter of explanation just in case. Do you know where his secretary is?'

'Phyllis?' the other looked out at the corridor. 'Well, she was here a minute ago.'

'Look, I'm very sorry,' said O'Ryan, 'but I can't stop. Could you tell her I called, and it was most urgent that I had to go. I'll put the letter explaining what's happening on her desk. Could you tell her?'

'Dear me, you are in a state!' said the other. 'Yes, I'll tell her.'

'Thanks!' said O'Ryan, and grabbed her shoulders impulsively.

As the secretary looked startled, O'Ryan hared again out of the door, back through the archway and the quad, and out through the porter's lodge.

A second later he dashed back in again, seized a letter addressed to him which he had glimpsed on the top of the pigeon-hole for the Os, and stuffing it in his green-corduroy-jacket pocket, hurled himself towards the High Street on his bicycle.

*　*　*　*

'And so I would recommend that all the books are sold,' said Snare. 'I don't see these sort of subjects ever coming back into favour. Even the primary texts of Classical works, old though they may be, will have been superseded by new editions, and as for the critical works — as I have indicated — most of them are just frightful.' Snare finished his report, and the sprawling dons looked lethargically over to Fobey again.

'May I just ask one thing?' said Harold Revere.

'Yes?' snapped Fobey.

'I'm not continuing the point about packing the committee or trying to be provocative, but why have we just had this report? If the Maeonides house hasn't been sold yet, why are we considering with such urgency what to do with its books?'

'Because they're here!' said Davenport.

'What do you mean here?'

'They're in the college, making a mess of the SCR library. You can't get anywhere near the shelves because the whole of Maeonides' library is all over the floor.'

'Is this so?' cried the earnest Mr Hapgood.

'I shall come to this matter in the report on the Maeonides house.'

'But why isn't Dr Werble giving a report on the house? I thought he was detailed to look into it. And he — if I may suggest it — is a man with considerably more interest in ancient texts and ancient history and mythology — even though it is not his field — than Dr Snare. I'm not casting aspersions on Snare, but why wasn't Dr Werble given the chance of examining the books?'

'Because Werble votes for the Hargreaves quad.'

'That is the last such insinuation I shall accept!' yelled Fobey. 'I am not going to sit here and be insulted in this way. That is the last time I am having these imputations made against me!'

There was a ghastly pause, while everyone stared at Fobey,

keenly aware that something had driven him into a state of nervous collapse.

Fobey swallowed, panted and tried to recover himself, 'I am appalled at the attitude of some of the fellows here.' He hesitated, swallowed, and started to grow maudlin. 'I called in Dr Snare because we want an up-to-date opinion on these books just as we need an up-to-date vote on this quad. I just happen to believe — and I resent anyone impugning the sincerity of my belief — that Oxford cannot live perpetually in the past. This university is not a theme-park. Nor is it a museum. It is a place of higher learning.'

'Ah no,' said Revere with suave irony, ignoring Fobey's distress. 'A museum is just what Oxford is and should be! I have always felt that Oxford should seek to be a museum that teaches by example: a living museum, working untrammelled by time. And we should equip our undergraduates with the museum-enshrined skills of learning, instead of sending them forth in a state of frenzied, virginal ineptitude.'

Sir Walter looked up. 'Well, Mr Revere, no doubt there are things to be said on both sides, but the question is not just one of ancient or modern styles. There are rather more practical things to attend to, and the Maeonides' inheritance is a case in point: a library stripped bare, a house ransacked and ravaged. I have reported to the committee that a television company has contacted me about permission to film in the house, and to read excerpts from the books of which we hold the copyright. I really feel we should consider restoring what has been squandered, and giving the house once more a living influence. But first let us —'

'I resign from this committee!' shrilled Dr Fobey, slamming his papers down. 'I resign! I refuse to take any more insinuations! I have served this committee faithfully and the college for four years. I will not stay here to suffer this character assassination!'

'Then let us slip in the vote on the quad,' said the President, 'before you go. I would hate Dr Fobey to feel we had forced the issue. Now, I understand that you have held an inconclusive vote ahead of the schedule published in the agenda. May I ask how the votes fell?"

'There were six for the Hargreaves plan,' said the secretary, 'and seven for the Hammerstein. Apart from your own vote pending, Mr Davenport has also not indicated his mind.'

'Then I suggest we press on with our discussions.'

Fobey stared ahead manically.

Everyone else settled in their seats.

*   *   *   *

Silently falling, sucked from the grey air, hushing like a theatre-curtain pulled over the ancient scene of the wrought-iron gate, the dark-mudded canal, the lamplit arcade of the New Buildings, from the round heaven down into the square, by delicate drifts that tripped with silver-leathered sandals, where the roofs grew white and the gargoyles pale, all over the soft-wheeled van and waggon, shopping-mall and double-decker bus, bouncing kid, skidding don, hurrying shopper, the snow came tumbling, snow cascading, snow in a storm of black and white, and the fingers of ghosts brought all to purity.

For noiselessly fell the snow on the deer-park, where the roes twitched puzzled ears, and the lights were burning in the Classical windows. And the snow fell quietly over the waterside beeches and cottages by the weir, softly rustling onto the rusty leaves. And the snow fell quietly over the quads and courts of St Mary's, blowing in the door of the incensed chapel. And the snow fell quietly over the breath-steaming O'Ryan as he pedalled by the river, and his bicycle wrote long lines on the road behind.

And when it fell on the old college scout, who was stacking chairs outside the JCR, he looked up and thought of calling in at the kitchens. And when it fell on the young don, who was taking exampapers to the office, he yearned to dash home to play with his young son at snowballs. And when it fell on the students walking, even those deep in arguments, and they tipped back their heads and felt the flakes on their faces, they thought of the fine-threaded hair of girls falling about their eyes, and yearned for warmth and deluge of love's sweetness.

And when it fell by the committee-room windows, the chairman was staring at the hands, and he and the secretary wrote down seven votes for Hammerstein. And when it fell on by the committee-room windows, the chairman was still staring, and he and the secretary wrote down seven votes for Hargreaves. And Davenport dallied, still undecided, sitting in the chintz window-seat, half in the warm and half lit by the cold.

But when he looked out at the teeming flakes of snow that were cast on the lawns, he had a vision strange and baffling to him, for he thought he saw a sledge hauled by deer, hung with black, with lanterns and incense, passing towards the archway and onto the road, and about the sledge a group of eight girls, dancing in Grecian tunics, with silver hands from great urns flinging snow. And the flakes teemed over the grey-limbed trees by the battlemented walls and he could not but smile at the ancient beauty. So he held up his hand, and eight votes were cast for the neo-classical quad. And at that moment the Muses sang.

*   *   *   *

With a feeling of glowing exhaustion O'Ryan cruised along Foxview Road, leaving the tense and bustling city behind. Through a vast snowy landscape in the heavy twilight he laboured, and felt he was approaching a final place of rest. The storm and the snow were like the time he had passed to this hour, but now he felt the dusk unfolding treasures. His fingers in his gloves were nipped hard by the frost, his face felt raw from the stinging wind. But his blood was warm, his clothes clung close, and he felt purged and cleansed as though from a deep sickness.

Just as he came to the place to turn into the drive of Number Eleven, he stopped and looked out over the hills towards the west. The country seemed to grow sandy that way, for pine-trees and firs abounded, and the tangled blackberry-thickets, now crisscrossed in snow, led the eye an austere journey towards purer plains. Here deep among resinny forests the foxes hopped through the snow, and the pheasant crowed cold in the evening oaks. The snow seemed to have levelled the world, swept away prejudice and ignorance, and mapped a way towards a clearer form.

O'Ryan biked into the garden of the house. The sky was golden beyond, but the porch and the windows were all steeped in dusky cold. He saw no lights burning anywhere, as he set his bicycle against the wall. But O'Ryan's heart did not fail. He was confident. The mere sound of Dr Alting's voice had changed everything. He got off his bike and unclipped his trousers. Then he went to the door where the porch had shielded the flags from snow, stamped his boots clear and rang the bell.

As before the bell failed to sound. O'Ryan tried the door. It was

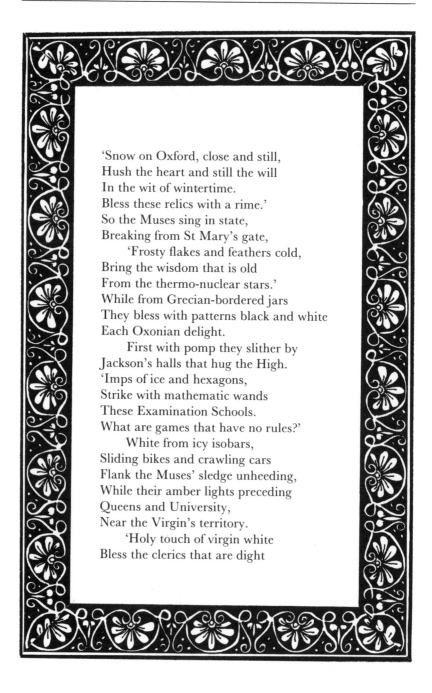

'Snow on Oxford, close and still,
Hush the heart and still the will
In the wit of wintertime.
Bless these relics with a rime.'
So the Muses sing in state,
Breaking from St Mary's gate,
          'Frosty flakes and feathers cold,
Bring the wisdom that is old
From the thermo-nuclear stars.'
While from Grecian-bordered jars
They bless with patterns black and white
Each Oxonian delight.
          First with pomp they slither by
Jackson's halls that hug the High.
'Imps of ice and hexagons,
Strike with mathematic wands
These Examination Schools.
What are games that have no rules?'
          White from icy isobars,
Sliding bikes and crawling cars
Flank the Muses' sledge unheeding,
While their amber lights preceding
Queens and University,
Near the Virgin's territory.
          'Holy touch of virgin white
Bless the clerics that are dight

By Isis, and the ancient stream
That wash the heels of academe.'
    Now through the eddies of the snow
See-through pink umbrellas go,
Close in Catte Street's narrow wedge
The sleigh-bells echo of the sledge,
Loud in lanes and high-walled streets
By Hertford's arched Venetian treats,
By All Souls' Turkestan-like towers,
By Radcliffe's dome, and stoney flowers
That sprout their hyacinths alone
On Bodley's linen-folded stone.
    'Trilling quavers of the snow,
Bless the music that they blow
In Sheldonian's tiered seat.
Give it heart and keep the beat!'
Thus they greet the concert-hall,
Where the Chancellor has his stall.
    'Tumbling deluge of the clouds,
Bless the books that Bodley crowds,
Or shops on shelves, and give them sense
To know their own inheritance.'
Here they pass the Broad along,
Where the Clarendon is strong.
    'Unifier of the form,
Wake again the skill that's drawn

In Ashmolean's rich show
Of painters canvassed long ago.
Or with their vanity a-gleaming
Bless the Thespians with redeeming:
Skill restore and power and grace
Of the Playhouse in its place,
Of the dancer in that dell,
Of the learned in their cell,
Of the prince and punter all
In the shop and shopping-mall,
That all Cornmarket attend
This the song with which we end.'

locked as before. He stood back and looked at the house. It did not seem to have changed since he came a day or two before. He went at once round the wall, and passed along the side, then pushing through the snow-heavy boughs of the clustering currant-bushes, stopped a while in amazement at the garden. All in white, untrodden and occult, it had rushed to join the secret purity, and now new, yet the same, was a chaste bride playful in radiance.

The conservatory was open. He creaked back its glass door. He went into the cold, damp house. There were no lights, but he did not doubt. There was no noise, but he sighed in the silence. It was empty and bare, yet what riches were held in that transfiguring place! He walked into the hallway. He looked in the study. He softly put his foot on the stair. With a sigh, he mounted the stairway to eternity.

With a footstep lighter than a mouse he came to the top of the stairs. Without noise he crossed to the door of the bedroom. He knocked softly. He opened the door. He looked in the twilit room. The lilac room, suspended in snow-purple. He looked for the bed. In the light of the snow, he saw the French bed still there. And a beautiful girl sitting back on its pillows. It was Miss Alting. She smiled at him tenderly with her head on one side. O'Ryan gazed and felt tears come to his eyes.

He walked towards her. Her smile was soft, yet dazzling in stillness and sweetness. She was patting the bed. He went to it and sat down.

'I began to think I should never be here and see you again,' he said. 'Such trouble and such doubt has been cast on our meeting! And the house so empty! Everything gone! I thought you might be too. But you are the very well of kindness. Your father rang and suggested I come since you are going away. He says you have the chance of a cure in America. He said I may come and bid farewell. But do you really plan to go tonight, in this darkness and in all this snow?'

Miss Alting smiled at him and gently nodded.

'And do you have to go so soon, with hardly a chance to talk?'

Miss Alting sadly smiled and softly nodded.

'And will you ever come again?' O'Ryan had tears in his eyes.

Miss Alting glanced down with a sigh.

Then he hurried on, not wanting to hear. 'But still: how can you go tonight?' he whispered. 'Look at the snow. The roads are hard and deep.'

She nodded, and gestured with her hands.

'Your father is coming to fetch you?'

She shook her head, then made strange gestures once more. She marked up from her head with the palm of her hand a succession of stages.

O'Ryan was baffled.

She did it again. She counted upwards, as though of a family.

O'Ryan gasped. 'Your brothers and sisters?'

She pointed to him as he said the latter.

'Your sisters are coming to fetch you?' O'Ryan laughed. 'I hope in a sledge!'

She pointed to him again on this last word.

O'Ryan laughed. He wanted to fling himself upon her and roll happily over the bed. She made a face of playful worry at this, as though she read his thoughts. O'Ryan seized her hands and with a sigh he leant down and kissed them. She looked at him kindly and stroked his hair. O'Ryan stared at her a long time. But again he could not bide her gaze. Such depth and kindness and love made him tremble.

She snatched up her note-pad and pencil.

O'Ryan happily watched her write, enjoying seeing her frown of concentration.

She showed him the paper. He read it eagerly. It said, 'I have something to tell you.'

O'Ryan nodded with admiration. 'What?' he said at last.

She took the pencil and wrote again eagerly. She held him the paper.

O'Ryan read it with amazement. It said, 'I can talk.'

'You can talk!' he shouted. Then he put his hand over his lips, as he heard the house echoing to his yell.

You can talk? he mouthed and gestured to her.

'Yes,' she said in a pure, low voice.

O'Ryan sat gazing at her, puzzled, for there was something so familiar in her voice, even though he had never heard it before.

At length he gestured frowning: how come?

She shrugged. 'I just seemed to have got better.'

O'Ryan gestured: right now?

She shrugged. 'Since we last met.'

O'Ryan shook his head and gestured: how?

She said, 'It was while I was reading your poems, all twenty-four of them, and enjoying them very much. But when I came across one that had got the quantitative metre all wrong, and it was also pretty stupid and big-headed, after all the ones I had enjoyed, and really thought were so lovely, I went huh! — And the next minute I found I could talk! It was from that little, let-down bump that I felt a sort of catch open, and I suddenly realised I couldn't let you get away with it.'

She was grinning now. O'Ryan started chuckling, then rolled over on the blankets, and stared up at the ceiling, laughing sweetly. She was in fits too. Together they shook in merry convulsions on the bed, until at last he rolled towards her and shook his head.

Then pressing his hand against his chest, he gestured to her lovingly, gesturing roundly to her fair face with his hand. Finally with a sigh, he slid forward on her lap, set his head on her thighs, and lay there with his arms wound about her.

She looked down at him tenderly, but then puzzled, gazing down at him, feeling something in his coat sticking sharply in her skin. She slipped her fingers inside his jacket. 'What's this?' she said frowning, and pulled out the unopened letter O'Ryan had snatched from his pigeon-hole on leaving college.

He gasped and nodded in recognition, rolled over and opened it up, then held it so that they could both read it. It said:

Dear Mr O'Ryan,
I am afraid I will have to postpone our meeting at four on Monday until tomorrow Tuesday morning at eleven. I should tell you, however, that your letter from Dr Alting is already in my hands. It came by means of a friend of yours anxious to excuse you from blame. I find it and various other evidence of your innocence satisfactory, and can therefore assure you that your place in Oxford is safe.
Yours sincerely,
Sir Walter Lawrence, President of St Mary's

They finished the letter silently together.

Miss Alting smiled, 'How charming of him to reassure you so soon. It seems any troubles you might have had are ended.'

O'Ryan looked at her wonderingly again, now passing beyond astonishment, as she folded up the letter and replaced it in his breast pocket.

'My dear,' she whispered, 'we cannot be long. Soon you must carry me down, because I fancy that my sisters will arrive presently. They are taking me away to the west, where cities and palaces lie, far off in the grey waves of the Atlantic. The gods that we have loved are there, guarding eternal truths. The seasons have turned and brought all to fulfilment. I shall be well in that blessed heaven, and strength will come again, and the long night of weakness and spite be forgotten. My dearest poet and knight,' she smiled at him lovingly, 'with your verse you have set free a Muse tongue-tied for too many years. From a wild, far place in Africa you came to my frozen lips, and you learnt for me the steps of the ancient dances. Since these things have made us one, do not grieve if we must part. There is a place where we are together. Remember me only, my sweet, as one that smiled on you in the garden, and keep a holy fire for me in your heart. Go then. Look out before the house, and quickly come again, and tell me, my dear, what you see.'

O'Ryan frowned and held out his hand.

'It must be,' she sighed. 'It must be. Go, quickly. Perhaps we can lie and talk a little.'

O'Ryan slid softly off the bed, and with salty tears in his heart, grieving went from the room and along the hall. Mauve glowed the window. The whole world outside was plunged in purple twilight. Heartbreaking was the beauty of the garden.

Then at first he thought he heard sleigh-bells, but peering hard into the night, he saw only flurries of snow swirling in the drive. They seemed to pour towards the house and then draw up in front of it, blurred and mysterious, and he did not know truly if they were there. He walked back thoughtfully to the bedroom.

She laughed. 'Well, you have seen something. Perhaps you will see more with me beside you.'

She held up her arms for him to lift her.

O'Ryan went forward and knelt at her feet. She paused and tenderly stroked his hair.

'O'Ryan!' she sighed. 'You know why you have the name of
O'Ryan? You are someone whom we all knew long ago. In ancient
times there was an Arion, a poet at the court of a king, who had an
adventure much like yours of today. Do you remember the legend
of how Arion's companions threw him out of their ship, because
they had had enough of his poetic enthusiasms? But just as you
were saved coming here, he was saved by the dolphins, when they
swam with Arion back to King Periander? Come,' she smiled, 'lift
me up. My sisters will only tease me. What are you doing in an
old house with a young poet?'

She put her soft hand round his neck. She slid into his arms. He
carried her from the room, down the stairs, along the passage.

But when they came to the front door, 'Wait,' she whispered.
'Now I must be strong. For now I go away from this home on a
long journey. Set me down where I can stand. Then leave me to
the air. Only look and touch no more.'

O'Ryan let her slide to the floor. She stretched out her legs with
pain. Then she stood and hesitantly walked towards the door.

When the door was opened, O'Ryan saw in the evening snow
and the dusk, burning with hanging lanterns a mighty pageant:
eight Grecian maidens with tendril-bordered chitons, standing
with crackling torches about an ebony, deer-harnessed sledge. A
perfume from the fire-brands came, fuming beneath snowy trees,
and the smoke coiled up to the figured stars. Draped in black
velvet, powdered in snow, the ornate sledge curved its runners,
decked out with carvings of jet like a royal coach.

O'Ryan felt a breeze before him. Moving from the doorwary
Miss Alting he saw transformed in health and wealth. She now
stood light on lovely legs. Her pale cheeks were now rose, her eyes
sparkled with a blazing star-light. In delicately flower-decked
peplos, pleated in a thousands grooves, with lillies and diamonds
stuck amongst her hair, she laughed with dazzling happiness, and
ran to her smiling sisters, and gathered them about her gleefully.

O'Ryan stared amazedly on those with strange ancient masks,
and those bearing learned scrolls or trumpets, on those with
flowers born in their hands, those with flutes, tongs, clocks, and
Miss Alting he saw now take up a lyre. She swept her hands
across the seven strings, and echoing, watery sounds twangled the
air from the tortoiseshell base. Then she slipped as if shivering

into the glossy sables on the sledge, covering herself to her neck against the cold.

O'Ryan saw her warm and snug, smiling from the snow-starred darkness. He could not hold his arms from a final embrace. He sighed, he reached. But his hands met nothing and grasped the empty air. With tears he saw her gaze from beyond his world.

Then with gentle clash of bells, the sledge was drawn by the maids on the ice. Antlered roebuck and white-spotted does led the winter triumph. And O'Ryan shuddered. His cheeks prickled over to see spirits move, drawing away from the old house on the hill. He watched them pass the snow-lined gateway, turn to the icy road, in a flickering procession fade from the winter garden.

O'Ryan took his bike. He wheeled it forward, leapt into the saddle, pedalled through the gate. But the sledge had moved too fast. O'Ryan sped over the ice to the road that led down to a view of the city. But the girls had gone. The moon lit the valley of snow.

The domes and turrets of Oxford burned with lights amidst the frost. And the holy pageants danced among the stars.

✓ 98
1 -

Snow p 208.